CHRISTMAS SURPRISES AT MERMAIDS POINT

SARAH BENNETT

Boldwood

First published in Great Britain in 2021 by Boldwood Books Ltd.

Copyright © Sarah Bennett, 2021

Cover Design by Alice Moore Design

Cover Photography: Shutterstock

The moral right of Sarah Bennett to be identified as the author of this work has been asserted in accordance with the Copyright, Designs and Patents Act 1988.

A CIP catalogue record for this book is available from the British Library.

Paperback ISBN 978-1-80280-925-1

Large Print ISBN 978-1-80280-924-4

Hardback ISBN 978-1-80280-930-5

Ebook ISBN 978-1-80280-927-5

Kindle ISBN 978-1-80280-926-8

Audio CD ISBN 978-1-80280-919-0

MP3 CD ISBN 978-1-80280-920-6

Digital audio download ISBN 978-1-80280-922-0

Boldwood Books Ltd
23 Bowerdean Street
London SW6 3TN
www.boldwoodbooks.com

This book is dedicated to Jessica Redland, with love and thanks x

1

A gust of wind swept in over the sea, sending the wild waves into an even bigger churning mass of foam as they raced into shore. Up over the narrow stretch of sand they surged, thundering over the pebbles and rocks that made up much of the beach at Mermaids Point. The blast of cold air battered against the shops lining the street overlooking the beach. Shutters rattled, and the wind's chilly fingers stole through air bricks and any tiny gap around the window frames, reminding the residents huddled inside that the full force of winter had settled its icy grip over the Point. The gust struck a lone figure hurrying along the footpath, trying to steal her hat from her head and making her grab for both it and the ends of the thick scarf she'd tied round her neck in a fruitless effort to keep warm. *So much for a White Christmas*, Nerissa Morgan thought, recalling the joy of the forecaster on breakfast TV as she'd shared image after image sent in by viewers of picture postcard snowscapes. Unlike the residents of the Point, most of the country had woken to a pristine blanket of white, and crisp blue skies, perfect for wintery walks and building snowmen in the back garden. Poor Max. The only thing her partner's teenage son was going to find at the bottom of their garden was a muddy quagmire. It was probably one of the last years when doing silly things like building snowmen still held appeal. He was already showing signs of shifting from the sweet, open boy who chased around with Toby, their golden retriever, into a hormone-fuelled teen.

The windows of her niece's café cast a warm, welcoming glow into the unrelenting gloom of the afternoon. Nerissa quickened her pace as another gust of wind sent a shock of icy raindrops into the small gap between the brim of her hat and the top of her scarf, stinging her cheek like a slap. She reached for the handle to the café and nearly stumbled as Laurie tugged it open from the other side. 'Come in! Oh, you poor thing, give me your coat and I'll hang it up. Linda said you were coming so I've been keeping an eye out for you.' At mention of her friend, Nerissa looked around until she spotted Linda and gave her a quick wave before allowing her niece to help her out of her wet outer layers.

The friendly chatter from this young woman, Nerissa couldn't have adored more if she were her own child, did as much to warm her as the toasty heat of the café's interior. Smiles of welcome greeted her from the handful of occupied tables, further cheering her mood. Barbara, Kitty and a couple of other members of the local knitting circle were gathered round a pair of tables which had been pushed together, needles flying as fast as their tongues as they nattered over the latest gossip. Jake, Laurie's other half and Linda's son, was hunched over his laptop at one of the little round tables by the window, head bouncing to whatever tune was pouring from the white earbuds into his ears as his fingers flew across the keyboard. 'Someone's busy,' Nerissa observed with a nod towards him as she surrendered her sodden coat and accepted a kiss on the cheek from her niece.

'Oh, don't get me started,' Laurie said in a voice full of exasperated affection. 'He's obsessed with an idea for a book, and I can't tear him away from that flipping laptop. I've told him if I see so much as a hint of it on Christmas Day I'm going to toss the bloody thing over the end of the Point.'

'Don't mention Christmas.' Nerissa pulled a face as she held up her hands to ward off mention of the day she was beginning to dread.

'Is everything all right?' Laurie placed an arm round her shoulder. 'I thought things were going well with Tom and the kids.'

Even with all the current stress, the mere mention of the ready-made family she had somehow found herself in the middle of filled Nerissa with a joy so all-encompassing, she struggled to contain it. Her old boss had retired at the end of the summer, and his replacement had taken over not only the doctor's surgery, but her heart as well. 'Oh, they are,' she reassured Laurie with a quick hug. 'I'm just so horribly unprepared for it all.' She hesitated, then gave Laurie a rueful smile. 'It's the first big celebration since Tom and I got together, and I want it to be perfect.'

'It'll be fine,' Laurie said with the kind of assurance Nerissa wished she could believe. 'They all adore you. Anyone with eyes can see how much both Emily and Max have settled into life here at the Point, and that's down to you as much as their father.'

'I hope you're right.' Nerissa shook her head at the creeping self-doubt and straightened her spine. 'I know you are. It's finding the right balance that's got me a bit worried, that's all. I want to honour the traditions they had when Anna was around, without anyone thinking I'm trying to replace her.' Tom's wife had died of cancer three years ago, and though the children were coming to terms with their loss, Nerissa still found herself tiptoeing across the high wire bridging the past with the future they were building together.

Luckily, Tom was the perfect safety net, ready to catch her when she inevitably stumbled as she had the previous weekend when she'd hung up the stockings she'd found in a box of decorations Tom had brought from his old home in London. They had looked hand decorated, the front of each one featuring a different festive character with a name stitched beneath them. A smiling Father Christmas for Tom, a cheery snowman for Anna, a red-cheeked elf for Emily and a nutcracker soldier for Max. She'd hung the other ones on the mantelpiece, setting Anna's carefully to one side so she and Tom could talk to the children about whether they wanted to hang it or not. Only they'd got caught up with an emergency in the surgery and the kids had arrived home from school and college respectively and seen the gap on the mantel before Nerissa could explain. There'd been a lot of slamming doors from Emily, and a smattering of tears from Max. Nerissa had felt like crying herself as she'd listened to Tom's careful negotiation with his daughter through her bedroom door. When he'd finally collapsed beside her in the king-size bed they now shared in his room, she'd wished, not for the first time, for the peace and safety of her little flat on the upper floor of the building that housed both the surgery and the family's living quarters. Life would be so much simpler if she'd kept her feelings to herself on the beach that fateful night when they'd feared something terrible had happened to Max. It was only ever a fleeting thought, a cowardly moment when the risk of what they were trying to build together felt too big. She loved Tom and the children with her whole heart and if things didn't work out, she didn't think she'd survive it. Pushing the horrid doubts away, she gave Laurie one more quick hug. 'Make us a pot of tea will you, darling?'

'Of course. I'll bring it over. I've tried a new recipe – cookies and cream gateau. Do you want a slice?' Laurie's eyes danced with a look of sheer temptation. 'Go on, you know you want to.'

It did sound heavenly. 'A sliver.' Nerissa held up her finger and thumb an inch apart.

'You'll want more than that when you taste it.' With a grin Laurie headed back towards the counter which dominated the back wall of the café. As she went to pass Jake's table, his arm snaked out to snare her round her waist and Nerissa couldn't help but smile as Laurie tumbled into his lap with a shrieking laugh. They were so free and easy together – something she hoped she and Tom would find their way towards in time. Not that she was big on public displays of affection, she would leave that to the younger generation. There were times she still found herself hesitant to reach for him – particularly when the children were present.

Something of the melancholy of the moment must've shown on her face because Linda was out of her chair and crossing to meet her. Holding out her hands in welcome, her eyes crinkled with concern as she asked, 'Is everything all right?'

Nerissa smiled as she took Linda's hands and gave them a squeeze before taking a seat at the table her friend had chosen tucked against the back wall. 'Everything's fine. I was just watching love's young dream over there.'

'Makes you sick, doesn't it?' Linda's voice brimmed with love as she glanced across the room at her son who was trying to hold a not-struggling-very-hard-to-get-away, laughing Laurie in place on his knee. They'd been estranged for a number of years, but mother and son were slowly finding their way to a relationship that suited them both. She watched them for another moment before turning her attention back to Nerissa. 'Speaking of love, how's the delectable Dr Tom?'

Nerissa laughed. 'He's gorgeous, and perfect in every way.'

'But...' There was an astuteness to the appraising way Linda raised one brow.

'I'm feeling a little overwhelmed,' Nerissa confessed. 'We just never seem to have any time to ourselves.' She shook her head. 'God, I sound terrible, don't I?'

'Not at all.' Reaching across the table, Linda patted her arm. 'You went from nought to sixty in the blink of an eye. Anyone can see the two of you are meant to be, but you still missed out on a lot of the normal courtship steps.'

It was true. Their first kiss on the beach had progressed straight to Tom's bed the moment the children were settled, neither he nor Nerissa able to stem the tidal wave of pent-up feelings they'd been hiding from each other for too long. After that first night it had seemed silly to go back to sleeping in separate beds, especially as the kids had been unphased by it. Besides, the bedroom was the only place they got to be alone together, despite the fact they lived and worked under the same roof. 'I'm missing a bit of the romance, I guess,' she mused as Laurie approached the table with a pot of tea, two huge slices of mouth-watering cake, and a fresh cup of coffee for Linda. They paused for a moment to thank Laurie and give the cake the moment of silent appreciation it deserved before they sank their forks in. As the combination of cream, rich fudgy chocolate and crisp biscuit base melted on her tongue, Nerissa felt her eyes roll back in her head. 'My God.'

'Oh, wow. That's better than sex,' Linda exclaimed as she dug her fork back into the cake for a second bite.

'Not quite, but close,' Nerissa found herself saying before clapping a hand over her mouth.

'Ha! Tell me more.' Linda waved her fork at Nerissa in an encouraging gesture.

'My lips are sealed.' Nerissa took another bite of her cake and sighed. It really was delicious. If there was enough left, she would get Laurie to box up three slices for Tom and the children to enjoy after dinner. A peace offering, not that one was needed, but still it would be nice to treat them all. 'Don't get me wrong,' she said to Linda, returning to their original topic of conversation. 'I've never been happier, and I wouldn't change things for the world...'

Linda made a sympathetic noise. 'It can't be easy juggling everything with the surgery and at home, and still finding time to focus on just the two of you.'

'Exactly.' Nerissa gave her friend a grateful smile. 'Anyway, enough about me, what's going on with you?'

Linda cast a quick look round then leaned a bit closer. 'I sold the house.'

'What?' Nerissa couldn't help the outburst, so excited was she about the news. Linda made a shushing motion with her hands as she shot another quick glance to where Jake was sitting. His full attention was once more glued to his screen, and he didn't so much as look their way. She doubted he'd hear anything over the music from his earbuds, but Nerissa kept her voice hushed anyway as she leaned closer and said: 'I knew you were thinking about it, but I didn't realise you'd even been in touch with an estate agent.'

Linda nodded, eyes bright with a mixture of emotions. There were a lot of unhappy memories tied up in the house she'd shared with her late husband, but it must still be tough for her to let it go.

'I called one at the beginning of November and arranged for them to get the spare key from my next door neighbour. He was very enthusiastic about the place and wanted to put it on the market straight away. He arranged for a cleaner to go and give the place a dust and polish and had it on the website within a week. I was grateful when he suggested the cleaner, because the thought of going back there filled me with dread.'

'Oh, I wish you'd said something.' It was Nerissa's turn to reach out and offer comfort. 'If you need someone to come with you and clear the place out, you only have to ask.' She thought about what she'd said, then shook her head. 'You don't even have to ask, because I'm not going to let you do it alone. Sylvia will come too.' Nerissa's sister-in-law had been instrumental in helping Linda in the aftermath of her husband Nigel's sudden death. She'd even persuaded Linda to join them in the Point and rent one of the holiday cottages so she didn't have to be alone as she came to terms with her loss. Nerissa knew Sylvia would be in complete agreement about helping their friend through this difficult step as she transitioned from her old life to one they hoped would see Linda make a permanent home in the Point.

'There's no need.'

Nerissa sat back, surprised at the surety in Linda's tone. 'You know it'll be no trouble,' she offered, worried Linda was putting too much of a brave face on things.

'I know,' Linda assured her. 'It's a young couple buying their first home so I told the agent they could have their pick of what's there of the furniture, kitchenware et cetera free of charge. Anything they don't want is being sorted out by a house clearance company. There's nothing in that house other than bad memories. I won't bring the burden of them into my new life.'

'Well, as long as you're sure.' She certainly sounded it. The transformation from the mousy, downtrodden woman Nerissa had first met into the confident, happy one she was delighted to call a friend had been little short of miraculous. It was like she'd been trapped in the tightly wound cocoon of Nigel's oppressive behaviour. Now she was finally free of him, Linda had metamorphosized into the person she was always meant to be. 'Have you told Jake?' She lowered her voice as she mentioned his name.

A flicker of uncertainty crossed Linda's face as she shook her head. 'That's one of the things I wanted to talk to you about.' She took a sip of her coffee as though needing to compose her thoughts, and then set it down. 'It's not just the house. I completed probate on Nigel's estate and received a substantial settlement from a life insurance policy he'd taken out when we were first married. I had no idea about it – he kept all that sort of stuff to himself.'

'Well, it's not like he didn't owe you something after all you put up with.' Though she'd never met the man, Nerissa had formed a very strong opinion about the late Nigel Smith, and there was nothing good about it.

Linda's mouth stretched into a swift, hard smile. 'You can say that again.' Her expression softened. 'Between that and what the sale of the house fetched, I'm well set up. More than well, really.' She sent another quick glance towards Jake. 'I want to give some of it to Jake and Laurie, but I'm not sure how he'll feel about it.' Linda picked up the pretty cloth napkin from beside her plate and began pleating it between her fingers. 'Things are much better between us, and I don't want to do anything that might rock the boat. I know the two of them are saving like mad for a deposit so they can buy a place of their own and I'd like to help them, you know? Because it's the first time in Jake's life that I feel I'm in a position to do so.'

'I think that would be a wonderful gesture.' Nerissa watched her niece as she exchanged a laugh with the knitting ladies while swapping the large teapot on their table with a fresh one. She'd worked so hard to make a success of the café and Jake was doing a lot of freelance work for the local papers as well as a few features he'd sold on to the nationals through his old mentor, Mac. Even so, things were as tough for them as any other young couple in the current economic climate. 'I can also understand why you feel reluctant, but I don't think there's any chance it will damage things between you and Jake if you make the offer.'

'But what if he says no?'

Reaching out, Nerissa removed the crumpled napkin from Linda's hand and gave her fingers a comforting squeeze. 'Then accept his answer with good grace and tell him the only thing that matters to you is that he is happy.'

'I just want things to be easier for them.' Linda sighed. 'I'll bite the bullet and ask him later.'

'What will you do with the rest of it?' Nerissa hadn't meant to blurt it out quite so directly, but she really wanted Linda to stay.

'That's the other thing I wanted to talk to you about.' Linda leaned down to rummage in her bag, drawing out a thick brochure which she placed on the table between them. The front of the glossy booklet showed a gleaming white cruise ship sailing on an azure blue sea.

'You want to go on a cruise?' It wasn't something that Nerissa had ever really thought about but as she began to leaf through the pages, past images of gorgeously dressed cabins and sumptuous plates of food she could certainly understand the appeal.

'A world cruise,' Linda said as she reached out and flipped the pages to one she'd folded the corner down on. 'Ninety-nine nights, sets sail in the new year. The ship is reserved for adults only, and look at the lovely cabin with its own balcony. Imagine sitting out there with a glass of wine as the ship sails into San Francisco harbour, or past the opera house in Sydney.' Linda's voice had taken on a dreamy quality, telling Nerissa she was already picturing herself doing exactly that.

'Have you booked it?'

Linda shook her head. 'I spoke to an agent this morning and there's a few cabins left.'

She sounded wistful, and though three months on a ship full of strangers seemed to Nerissa like a heck of an undertaking; Linda had certainly taken turning over a new leaf to heart. If she felt ready to tackle another new adventure, Nerissa would do what she could to support her.

Nerissa scanned the entertainment pages, thinking carefully about what to say. It certainly looked like they had plenty to keep guests occupied. 'They have loads of dance classes,' she said with a grin as she pointed to a picture of a smiling older woman being guided through some steps by a handsome dance instructor. 'Who knows, you might get a Patrick Swayze lookalike!' Linda had joined a local salsa group not long after she'd first arrived, and the regular classes had trimmed her figure as well as given her a fantastic boost in confidence.

'More like Anton du-bloody-Beke, knowing my luck,' Linda muttered, sending them both into a fit of giggles.

'There's guest lecturers, too. And cookery classes with celebrity chefs,' Linda said, once they'd regained their breath. Taking the brochure from Nerissa she flipped through the next couple of pages until she found a photo of one of Britain's most illustrious chefs. 'And the travel agent told me they have a specific programme for single travellers with regular get togethers to help make a few friends. They said I'd be surprised how many people travel on their own, and that I shouldn't worry about that side of things at all.'

Swallowing any remaining doubts, Nerissa grinned at the enthusiasm in Linda's voice. It was clear she already had one foot in the cocktail lounge. 'You sound really keen.'

'I am,' Linda admitted with a shy grin. 'I really fancy escaping for a bit of sunshine.'

Nerissa cast a quick look at the sullen sky outside. She didn't blame Linda for wanting to get away. The Point was wonderful in summer when it was all blue skies and barbecues in the garden, but the winters could be grim and unrelenting. The long-range forecast was promising this would be a memorable winter, for all the wrong reasons. Three months trapped in a cottage on her own, or out exploring what the world had to offer? It was a no-brainer. 'So, what are you waiting for?'

Linda's grin widened into a broad beaming smile. 'You're right! What *am* I waiting for?'

2

'Daddy?'

At the sound of his daughter's voice echoing down the corridor, Tom Nelson tossed down the pen he'd been using to scribble down a Christmas to-do list, grateful for the distraction. Rising, he shoved his chair back a little harder than was strictly necessary, sending it skidding across the laminated floor. 'In here,' he called, heading out of his office to intercept Emily in the waiting area of the surgery next to Nerissa's empty reception desk. They had very few appointments booked so he'd told her he could handle everything for the afternoon, wanting her to have a break. When she'd given him a frazzled smile, he'd known the chances of her taking the time off to rest were slim-to-none, so he'd sent a surreptitious message to Linda, who'd been more than happy to invite Nerissa for a coffee and a catch up.

He'd been conscious that too much of the holiday preparations had fallen to Nerissa and he was determined to pull his weight more. Hence the very long list of outstanding tasks back on his desk. None of them were huge, but, when viewed as a whole, the prospect of getting through them all in time seemed impossible. His father, step-mother and half-brother, Alex, were coming down next week to avoid the worst of the traffic, and, supposedly, to help. Adding another three people to the mix just felt like a recipe for disaster. More mouths to feed, more opinions voiced, more decisions endlessly debated. If Tom could get a handle on things today he hoped he could head things off in advance by allocating specific jobs to people.

That was the theory, at least.

Emily stared up at him, looking so much like her mother it sent a pang through Tom. Nothing like the devasting pain of when Anna had first passed from their lives, though. More a distant echo, a shadowed regret that she was missing seeing this miraculous child of theirs grow into a vibrant, beautiful young woman. When she moved next to him and put her arms round his waist, Tom paused for a second to drink in the moment of easy affection before curling his arms round her back and pressing a kiss to the top of her head. 'What's up, sweetheart?' Tom asked.

Emily gave him a tight squeeze then pulled away just as quickly as she'd hugged him. Releasing her was tough, because the urge to hold on to both her and Max had been something he'd struggled with since the day Max had got himself trapped in one of the caves beneath the Point. Cut off by the rising tide, without the help of Nerissa's family – and many others in the Mermaids Point community – Tom might have lost him. He still woke up in a sweat some nights, arms flailing from where he'd been pulling himself through the endless churning water of a nightmare, Max always just beyond the reach of his fingertips. Only the comfort of Nerissa's soft voice in the dark, the welcoming warmth of her body as she held him close could chase away the demons of his greatest fear.

He shoved his hands in his pockets to counter the need to

reach for Emily, and even went so far as to take a half step back, conscious it was something he needed to work through without either scaring or smothering the children. God, it was hard though.

'Where's Nerissa?' Emily glanced round the empty waiting area as though Nerissa might pop up from behind one of the chairs. Tom felt something inside relax a little. It was the first time she'd actively sought Nerissa out since the debacle over the Christmas stockings. While Emily had been polite and well behaved since they'd all apologised for the misunderstanding, there'd been a lingering tension between the two which Tom had longed to fix. He'd kept his mouth shut, though, knowing anything he tried to do to hurry things along would likely backfire. It looked like his patience had paid off.

'She's having a coffee with Linda. She's been working really hard with all the Christmas stuff, so I wanted to give her a break. I'm trying to sort out a list of outstanding jobs to do, maybe you can give me a hand with that?'

'That's what I wanted to talk to her about – you as well.' Emily glanced round again looking slightly at a loss. 'I thought you'd both be here...'

'I'm sure she won't be long,' Tom said, curiosity piqued. 'Can it wait?'

'Not really.' Emily sighed. 'That'll teach me to try and arrange a surprise.'

'A surprise?' Tom's heart quickened at the idea. 'What sort of surprise?'

'Come through and I'll show you.' Emily tilted her head back down the corridor towards the door which separated the surgery from the family part of the building.

Tom glanced at his watch. His next appointment wasn't due for another ten minutes. 'Lead the way.' When they entered the kitchen, it was to find a beaming Max standing expectantly next to the rucksacks the children both used as school bags. Their coats and boots were stacked neatly next to the bags as though in preparation for a trip. 'Going somewhere?' Tom asked, unable to keep the surprise from his voice.

Max nodded, still grinning. 'Were staying with Uncle Andrew and Aunt Sylvia for the weekend.'

Tom wasn't quite sure how the kids had come to call Nerissa's brother and sister-in-law 'uncle' and 'aunt' but everyone seemed happy about it, so he'd let it go. Anything that gave them more security, a sense of family and certainty the adults in their lives could be counted on, was just fine by him.

'Are you now?' Intrigued, Tom turned to Emily. 'Is this part of your surprise?'

She nodded, looking very pleased with herself. 'We decided the two of you needed some time together without us hanging around. We're taking Toby with us.' The golden retriever wagged his tail from his basket in the corner, as though in agreement with the plan.

'That way you can snog each other whenever you like!' Max chipped in with a cheeky grin. Tom laughed, delighted – and slightly appalled – that his children had discussed his private life and found it wanting in some way.

'There's champagne in the fridge,' Emily said as she crossed to open the large appliance in the corner and show him. 'And a plate of antipasti from the deli, and chocolate covered strawberries.'

'Aunt Sylvia's work?' Tom guessed. He loved the sparky little red-head to bits, and he could imagine her delight at being given the chance to meddle.

'Yes.' Emily took his hand. 'We're not finished yet.'

'What else?' Tom laughed, letting Emily lead him towards the lounge, a giggling Max in tow. As they entered the room he stopped in his tracks and surveyed the gorgeous scene before him. His little Christmas elves had been busy. Candles and tealights covered every surface, and strings of fairy lights had been looped round the curtain poles. The coffee table, which usually filled the centre of the rug in front of the fireplace, had been pushed against one of the walls, leaving an open area in the centre of the room.

'So you can dance,' Emily said. 'I've made you a playlist.' Her fingers flashed across the screen of her smartphone and a second later the one in his pocket beeped to notify him he had a message. 'Uncle Andrew helped me with that, because I know you prefer oldies.'

Tom wanted to protest, but his musical preferences were rooted deeply in the 80's and 90's, so she probably had a point. 'You've been very busy.'

'And there's this,' Max said from where he was standing next to the mantelpiece, beaming with pride.

When Tom spotted the stocking with a smiley, red-nosed reindeer and Nerissa's name embroidered across it, a lump formed in his throat, and he had to blink to focus through the tears swimming across his gaze. 'Oh, you guys.'

Emily's arm curled round his waist. 'Do you like it?'

'It's...' Tom cleared his throat, laughed, and tried again. 'It's perfect.' He pressed a kiss to her cheek. 'You're perfect.' He held out his free arm to his son who cuddled in on the other side. 'You're both perfect. Thank you.'

'Ivy made it for us. I took Mummy's stocking with me, so she'd know the right style to make.' Emily unhooked herself and bent to pick up something he hadn't noticed sitting in the corner of the fireplace. 'And she made this.' She handed the fuzzy brown toy to Tom, who could only stare in wonder at it.

'It's called a memory bear,' Max said as he stroked a hand over the jumper the teddy bear was wearing with a snowman on the front and the word 'Anna' written beneath it.

'We used Mummy's stocking. I hope you don't mind?' Emily sounded suddenly anxious. Tom shook his head, too choked to speak.

'And see these?' Max picked up the teddy's left leg and showed Tom.

The bear had cream crocheted pads on each limb, and he recognised the significance of it immediately.

'Ivy used the bit she had to cut off Emily's blanket when she repaired it,' Max said, touching the pale paw with careful fingers.

Memories swirled in Tom's head, so vivid, he couldn't speak for a long moment. Anna had made the blanket when she'd been expecting Emily and had used it when nursing both the children, and later as a comforter whenever they'd been poorly. Max had accidentally ripped it when he'd taken it from his sister's room without asking. Nerissa had found someone to repair it – and helped to repair the rift between the children in the process. Thanks to Ivy's miraculous skills with needle and thread, the blanket had been restored to the bottom of Emily's bed, with a pretty satin trim that would hopefully protect the delicate material from any future damage.

'I can see that,' Tom said, finding his voice at last. 'It's wonderful.'

'I thought I might keep the bear in my room,' Max said, his not-quite-a-man voice gruff. 'After Christmas.'

'I think that's a great idea.' Tom gave the bear's head a final stroke before handing it back to his son. 'Why don't you put it back where it belongs for now, though?' As he watched Max place the bear carefully back in the corner by the fireplace, Tom knew he owed Ivy more than he could ever repay. She'd found a way to keep Anna's memory a part of Christmas, turning what had been a heartbreaking reminder of presents that would never be given into a little guardian who would watch over, not only the festivities, but their son too, for as long as he felt the need.

Thanks to a quick message from Linda, who'd been such a sport and managed to keep Nerissa away for a couple of extra hours, Tom had everything in place by the time he heard the back door open. 'I'm in the lounge,' he called out.

'I'm sorry I took so long, but you'll never guess what! Linda's only got it into her head to go on a world cruise, and she wanted me to go back to hers and help her with the booking. Oh!' Still unwinding her scarf from round her neck, Nerissa froze in the doorway much as Tom had done earlier. She looked from the flickering candles to the ice bucket holding the champagne on the coffee table to the single red rose Tom held outstretched towards her. '*Oh.*'

'Much as I'd like to take all the credit, you have the kids to thank for most of it.'

'Oh.'

Tom laughed. 'Is that all you've got to say for yourself?'

'What? Oh, I mean, no! Where are they – the kids?' She still hadn't moved from her spot by the door.

'They're with Andrew and Sylvia. Toby, too.' Tom took a step closer.

Nerissa's raven hair spilled over her shoulders in a wild tangle of curls, her cheeks two bright spots of colour from the freezing temperature outside and the hint of a blush as her gaze danced once more round the room before settling back on him. She looked beautiful, and not all-together of this world, like a siren who'd called to him from the deep and stolen his heart irrevocably. He wanted her so much, his entire body ached with the tension of it.

'They'll be gone for the whole weekend,' he added, letting the anticipation of the moment deepen his voice.

'*Oh.*' The scarf dropped from her fingers as he closed the distance between them and stroked her cheek. 'Tom.' Her voice had that dreamy quality, all desire and welcome that never failed to set his blood pumping.

'You're beautiful,' he whispered as he leaned forward to trace the soft skin of her jaw with his lips. 'So beautiful.' He pressed a kiss to her half-parted lips. 'And mine.'

'Yes. Always.' It was the promise she'd made him that night on the beach when he'd gone from suffering one of the worst moments of his life to experiencing one of the best.

'I've spoken to them about it, and Andrew and Sylvia are more than happy to have the kids stay with them one weekend a month from now on.' Tom gave a silent prayer of thanks to the generosity of the Morgan family as he reached for the buttons on Nerissa's cardigan and started to undo them.

'That sounds like a very good idea.' Nerissa's voice was a little breathless as she began to fiddle with the buttons on his shirt.

'I thought so.' He bent to kiss the hollow at the base of her throat. 'And Dad's going to take them for February half-term. I'll book a locum and we can spend the entire week in bed.'

'The entire week?' She abandoned the last few buttons of his shirt and reached instead to tug the end of his belt free. Her fingers teased the rigid length of him making him arch into her. 'Are you sure you'll be up to it?'

With a laughing growl he nipped the lobe of her ear with his teeth. 'I'm very sure. Wait until you hear what I've got planned for the summer holidays.'

Her husky laugh was better than any aphrodisiac as he yanked her T-shirt free from her waistband. He dragged the garment over her head, sending her curls flying and the plump sweetness of her breasts bouncing beneath the lace-edged camisole she was wearing underneath it. *How many layers of clothing did one woman need?* He was out of patience, his fingers rough as he dragged one thin strap down to reveal more of her creamy skin. Thoughts of sipping champagne, of slow dancing before the fire and sweet, slow seduction were all abandoned in the face of his need. That could wait for the next round.

Or the one after that.

He popped open the button of her jeans, followed the zip down until he was on his knees before her, the denim pooled round her ankles. He paused a moment to capture her eyes, reading only desire and a need to match his own in them. Satisfied she was with him all the way he leaned forward and touched his lips to the soft skin of her belly.

'Oh,' she said. Followed by 'yes,' and 'please,' and then neither of them needed any more words.

3

JAKE

Jake paused outside the door to the little cottage his mother had been renting in one of the small winding streets that splayed out from the main seafront in a higgledy-piggledy pattern that would give any modern day planner nightmares. She knew he was coming; he'd texted her not ten minutes ago to confirm he was on his way. He even had the spare key she'd given him in case of emergencies, and yet still he found himself knocking rather than letting himself in. His knuckles had barely grazed the wood before the door opened to reveal his mother's smiling face. 'That was quick,' he said, stepping back in surprise.

Linda laughed. 'Don't worry, I wasn't lurking in the hall waiting for you, I've just this second come downstairs.' She gave a little shiver as the cold air whipped in behind him. 'Come in before we let all the heat out.'

Although it was the first dry morning they'd had in ages, Jake still removed his shoes as he unzipped his jacket, a habit ingrained in him from when he'd been a very small boy. Linda glanced down at his socks and laughed at the sight of his Santa-clad feet. 'Very festive.'

He grinned, wiggling his toes. 'Andrew got them in for the shop and gave me a couple of pairs to try. Market research he called it.' Likely, Laurie's big-hearted dad had just wanted to give him something that would make him smile. Having a positive father figure was still as much of a novelty to Jake as silly Christmas socks, but he was slowly getting used to the idea that he had someone he could turn to. Someone more than willing to listen when he needed it, to offer a shoulder or a bit of friendly advice. To just be there.

'Well, I think they're rather fetching. Come on through to the kitchen, the kettle's not long boiled.'

Though he followed his mother down the narrow hall to the small kitchen at the rear of the cottage, the last thing he wanted was any more coffee. 'I've been up since four-thirty trying to finish off an article so if I have any more caffeine I won't sleep for a week.'

Linda turned to face him, an expression of concern creasing the skin round her eyes. 'Oh, you should have said something when I messaged you! I didn't mean to drag you away from your work.'

Jake swallowed a sigh at her reaction. She was still so worried about doing or saying the wrong thing around him. He knew it was a hang-up after years of being under his father's thumb, but it bothered him nonetheless. Knowing it was something only time could fix, he offered her a reassuring smile. 'It's all right, Mum. I'd all but finished it last night but I couldn't quite get the ending I wanted. It happens like that sometimes and I have to let my brain chew on it for a few hours. When I woke up, it had all fallen into place, so it was just a case of tweaking things round and rewriting a few paragraphs and a new ending.' He hesitated, then decided the best way to make things easier between them was to tell her the truth in his heart. 'Even if I hadn't finished it, it wouldn't matter. You said you had something you wanted to talk to me about. I'm always going to come if you need me.'

'But you're so busy, and Laurie must be flat out as well with all the last-minute orders. I should've thought about that.' She waved a hand as though dismissing the idea that anything she wanted could be a priority.

Pulling out a chair, Jake sat and rested his forearms on the table. 'Tell me.'

After taking a few moments to make herself a cup of tea, Linda settled in the seat opposite him. 'I...' She looked away eyelashes fluttering madly as though she was fighting back sudden tears. 'Goodness, I don't know why this is suddenly so hard.'

Jake reached out and placed a hand on her arm. 'It's going to take time, Mum.' They'd been estranged for most of his adult life, since Jake had left home to go to university with his father's instruction not to darken his doorstep again ringing in his ears. He'd held him at his word, and had not set foot in the small suburban semi he'd been raised in until after Nigel Smith had been felled by a massive heart attack. Poisoned by his own spite and malice, more like it, because Jake wasn't sure his father had ever had a heart.

Linda laid her other hand on the back of his and took a deep breath. 'Okay. I'm going to say something, and I'd like you to listen to all of it before you respond. I also want you to know that whatever you choose to do about it is one-hundred percent fine with me.'

Not sure he liked the sound of that, Jake sat back a little in his seat, but he left his hand resting beneath hers in support. 'Okay...'

'There's a couple of things. First of all, I'm going away in the new year for a few months. I've always wanted to travel more so I've booked myself on a world cruise.'

Jake was surprised at the idea because she'd never struck him as the adventurous type. Then again she'd never struck him as the salsa dancing or open water swimming type either, but she'd tried and enjoyed both those activities over the previous couple of months. His mother was on something of a voyage of self-discovery and if translating that from metaphor to reality was part of it then he had no objections. Still, he wasn't ready to let her go sailing off into the wide blue yonder until he'd seen the details of the trip and assured himself she had everything in place in case of an emergency. 'Can I ask a couple of questions about that, or do you want me to wait?'

Linda smiled. 'My son, the journalist.' She said the words with deep affection. 'I should've known better than to expect you to wait – ask away, but my mind is made up about this at least.'

Jake patted her arm, pleased she felt confident enough to assert herself. 'I'm not questioning your decision, just interested in hearing more about your plans.' He hesitated as another thought occurred to him. 'What are you going to do about this place?' He gestured around to indicate the cottage. Leaving it lying empty for several months seemed like a waste of money.

The smile lighting her face dimmed as her expression settled into something more serious. 'I've agreed with the owner that I'm going to hand it back. They want to do some maintenance over the winter, anyway, and Nerissa has said I can store anything I need to with them at the surgery.'

Jake wondered for a moment why she hadn't asked him, and was surprised at the little pang of hurt that accompanied the thought. It didn't take more than a second or two to dismiss the silly feeling. The little cottage he and Laurie lived in on the top of the Point was comfortable enough, but it couldn't compare in terms of space to the sprawling building that housed both the surgery and Tom and Nerissa's family. Naturally it made sense for his mum to keep her things there. 'And what about when you come back?'

'While I'm away, I plan to do a lot of thinking about the future. And that includes deciding whether or not I want to come back to the Point, or if it's time to make a fresh start on my own.' She must've seen him open his mouth because she held up a hand and he closed it again. She'd asked him to listen, and he was doing a terrible job of it so far. 'You and Laurie, and everyone else have been so kind and welcoming to me when none of you had any cause to show me kindness.' She swallowed again. 'I let you down, Jake, and I don't know if that's something I can ever get past. I look at you now, at the strong, compassionate man you've become and I'm so proud of you. But I also know that you've become the person you are in spite of me and your father, not because of us and that shames me.'

This time he couldn't keep quiet. '*Mum.*'

She squeezed his hand to acknowledge she'd heard the protest in his voice, but she ploughed on regardless. 'You and Laurie deserve the space and time to build what I hope with all my heart will be a joyful and long life together. I feel like the spectre at the feast, a shadow of the past you shouldn't have to have hanging over you when you should be putting all your time and attention into your future.'

Jake closed his eyes against the pain and regret in those words. It was true he'd had a lot of misgivings about opening his life back up to her, but having the example of the Morgan's to show him what a family could be together, he'd found himself wanting that for him and his mum as well. He opened his eyes, caught his mum's gaze, and held it when she might have glanced away. 'And if I said I wanted you to be part of that future?'

'Then I'd say you were the very best of men, but I'm still not sure if it's enough to change the way I feel.' She leaned across the table towards him. 'I don't ever want us to lose touch, and I promise that, going forward, I will be as involved with your life as you want me to be. I'm just saying it might be better for you - for both of us - if I do that from a distance.'

Jake shook his head. 'I don't understand.'

Linda sighed. 'I'm not sure how I can explain it other than to say I spent too many years letting your father control my life.'

'I'd never try to do that!' Jake protested hotly, feeling almost sick that she could even think it.

Linda shook her head. 'I know. That's not what I'm saying at all.' She blew out a long breath. 'God, what am I trying to say? Your father couldn't have taken as much control as he did unless I was willing to surrender it to him. There were times early on when if I'd stood my ground things might have been different, but I didn't. I let him take charge because it seemed the easy choice. I went pretty much from my parents looking after me to your dad. I can't put myself in a position where I might let you do the same thing. It's time I took responsibility for myself and my own happiness.'

Jake let that sit for a while. His immediate response was to protest that he wouldn't let it happen, but was that true? Deep down he knew he'd walked away because that too had been an easier path. He could've stood up to his father as an adult, could've tried to help his mum leave him, but he'd done neither of those things. If anything, the guilt he carried over it had only grown stronger these past months as he'd watched Linda strike out on her own. The more she came into herself and out of his father's shadow, the more he berated himself for not doing something sooner. 'I wish I'd helped you.'

Linda's smile was soft and sad. 'And I wish I'd never made you feel like you needed to help me.' She sighed. 'If wishes were horses, beggars would ride as my grandmother would say.

We are where we are now and it's time for us both to move forward.'

She pulled her hands away from his and sat back, folding her arms across her chest in what could only be described as a defensive gesture. 'And now to the final thing I want to talk to you about.' The next words came out in a rush, as though she was worried he'd jump in before she could get them all out. 'I've sold the house.'

Jake bolted upright. 'You have? When?' A wave of mixed emotions swept through him, taking him by surprise. Walking back through the front door following his father's death had been one of the hardest things he'd had to face. He should be glad to know he'd never have to do it again, and yet? He shook the whisper of regret off. Hopefully, whoever had bought it would be able to fill the place with much happier memories than the ones he'd been left with.

'All you need to know is that it's done and dusted. Between that and a life insurance policy he had; your dad has left me quite well off. I want you and Laurie to have some of it. Enough to put down a deposit on a place of your own.'

His immediate gut instinct was to reject the idea. He didn't want anything from his father. Not now, not ever. 'We don't need it.'

Linda raised a sceptical brow. 'You're telling me that things are easy for the two of you, with you working for a local paper and Laurie trying to run a business that relies on regular tourist income? Sylvia told me how hard it was when the previous couple of summers were mostly a washout.'

Okay, she had a point there, but even so. 'I don't want it.'

'And if the source of the money wasn't tainted? If it was Andrew and Sylvia who were in a position to make such an offer? Don't cut off your nose to spite your face, Jake.'

Well, shit. She had him well and truly skewered on the sharp end of her point. 'Won't you need it?'

She shook her head. 'I've got enough to look after myself for now, and to support me through any training I do.'

'Training?' Jake clutched at his head, mostly as a joke, but the amount of stuff she was throwing at him was enough to send it spinning. 'You're not doing things by half, are you Mum?'

Linda laughed. 'I can't sit around on my backside for the rest of my life. I've no idea what I want to do, only that I want to do *something*. It's one of the things I'm hoping to work out while I'm away.'

'You'll be a whole new woman, soon.' Jake was impressed with how much she seemed willing to take on.

Refusing to be deflected for long, Linda leaned forward once more. 'Will you at least talk to Laurie about the money? As I said at the beginning, I'll abide by whatever decision you choose to make. I just want you to be sure you're making it for the right reasons. I know I can't change the past and that no amount of money will make up for what your father put you through, but he's gone and you're here and I want to see you thrive.'

It was Jake's turn to sigh. 'I know what you're saying. I'm just not sure if I can accept it.' Though it had been a terrible struggle at times, Jake was proud of the fact he'd earned everything he counted as a personal success through sheer graft. Leaving home and cutting ties with his parents had certainly made him self-sufficient, but it had also enhanced a natural tendency towards isolation. His inability to trust had almost cost him his relationship with Laurie.

Although his first instinct was to reject anything to do with his father, he owed it to the promise he'd made to be more open with Laurie to at least talk it through with her before he made any final decision. 'I'll think about it.'

'That's all I wanted to hear.' Rising from her seat, Linda came and stood beside his chair. Leaning down, she curled an arm round his shoulders as she pressed a kiss to the top of his head. It was something she used to do a lot when he was a kid and Jake found himself leaning into her just as he had then. He would let her go off round the world if that would make her happy, and he'd support her through what would be a difficult transition from homemaker into building a career for herself. As for leaving the Point for the long term? That he would fight tooth and nail because he wasn't going to lose her, not when things were just coming right between them.

4

If she never saw another mince pie it would be too bloody soon, Laurie thought to herself as she opened the oven door and turned her face away to avoid a blast of heat. Offering homemade Christmas fayre had seemed an ingenious way to supplement the waning income from the café over the quietest months, but she hadn't banked on it being quite so popular. She'd had orders for over two dozen Christmas cakes, alone. At least she'd been able to make them back in October and feed them a spot of brandy to keep them moist. She'd organised a couple of decorating work-shops for people who'd wanted to ice their own which had proven to be great fun for all involved, as well as adding a few more pounds to the coffers.

The past couple of weeks, though, had been a constant battle to keep the café ticking over as well as find time to prepare and bake enough batches of sausage rolls, mini quiches and mince pies to fulfil all the other orders. From the number of people who'd taken advantage of her services, Laurie suspected she could walk into most houses in the Point on Boxing Day and find something she'd baked on the buffet table. For all her silent complaining, she was delighted with the response really, and had already had a couple of enquiries from people about whether she might offer something similar for one-off events such as birthdays and anniversaries.

It was an idea she'd toyed with before and she planned to spend some time over the Christmas break working up a proper menu and costings. She'd played it a bit by ear this time round and had been able to maximise a profit by cooking larger batches. She paused in the act of removing a baking tray from the oven to turn her face into her shoulder and smother a yawn. Or perhaps she would spend the ten days she planned to close the café curled up in bed with Jake, dozing, catching up on boxsets they'd missed, and making love.

'What are you smiling about?'

Startled, Laurie managed to catch the tray before the mince pies did more than slide about. She placed it hurriedly on the counter before turning to where Jake was leaning against the doorway between the kitchen and the rest of the café. 'I was thinking about some of the plans I have for us over Christmas,' she said with a grin.

'Oh, I like the sound of these plans.' Jake crossed the room and slipped his arms round her waist, heedless of the pastry and flour smears on the front of her apron. 'Tell me more.'

'Well...' She let the word drag out a little until he coaxed a soft giggle from her by planting a kiss on the side of her neck. 'I thought we could take lots of fortifying walks along the beach. And the café could do with a spruce up, maybe a fresh lick of paint, even. It's not the sort of thing I can do when I'm open for business.' She wanted to keep the pretence up for longer, but his crestfallen expression was too delicious, and she collapsed into giggles against his chest.

'Witch,' he said fondly as he tightened his arms round her and pressed a kiss to the top of her head. 'You had me going there for a moment.'

Laurie snuggled closer, all thoughts of mince pies and sausage rolls forgotten. 'I've already told Mum we're spending Christmas Day just the two of us.' There'd been a couple of grumbles, but this was their first one together and she wanted it to be special. Besides, though she was used to the chaos and noise of her boisterous family, Jake's upbringing had been very different to hers. He cherished the times when it was just the two of them – as did she.

'And she didn't mind?'

The concern she heard in his words only made her hug him tighter, because as much as she knew he liked things more peaceful, he understood what her family meant to her. 'Honestly, I think she was putting it on for effect and is secretly relieved. Dad's plans for Boxing Day are getting out of control, especially now Nerissa and Tom are bringing their lot. If you add on Uncle Tony and his partner and your mum there's going to be sixteen of us.'

Jake's brow furrowed as he did a mental tally. 'Sixteen?'

She laughed. 'I was counting Toby as well.' Because her aunt's gorgeous retriever was as much a part of their extended family as any of the human members.

'Of course!' Jake's smile slid a little. 'Speaking of Mum...'

Sensing what was to come might be a bit sensitive, Laurie unhooked herself from Jake's hold and turned to the sink to wash her hands. 'I need to get on with boxing these orders, do you mind if we chat while I work?'

Taking his cue from her, Jake followed her to the sink and washed his hands as well before taking up station on the opposite side of the big workbench in the centre of the room. 'What do you want me to do?'

'There's a duplicate copy of each order there.' Laurie pointed to a neat stack of papers. 'Can you double check the contents of each box, close them and tape the order to the top?' She'd already made a start on packing some, so he had enough to get started with while she boxed up the next batches from the cooling racks. They worked in silence for a few minutes before she realised Jake had done his usual trick of disappearing off into his head. He did that a lot, and she knew if she didn't draw him out he'd chew over whatever was bothering him until he'd tangled himself into a knot of overthinking and indecision. 'So, what did your mum want to talk to you about?'

Jake waited until he'd finished checking the order in front of him and had secured the order sheet to the top of the box. 'She's taking herself off on a world cruise.'

'Wow.' Laurie wasn't sure what she'd been expecting him to say, but it wasn't that. 'Is she going on her own?' Linda had come out of her shell a lot in the months since they'd brought her back to the Point with them, but it was still a surprise to think about her taking on such a big adventure by herself.

Jake nodded. 'She talked it all through with Nerissa before she booked it and she's found a couple of cruise forums online where you can meet people who are planning to go on the same voyage. She's already made a few tentative plans to meet other single travellers for a drink on their first night on board.'

'Well, good for her.' Laurie loved everything about the sea, and she found herself wondering what it might be like to wake up in the morning and open the curtains to find your ship docked in a new city, or out in the middle of the ocean with nothing as far as the eye could see. It held a lot of appeal.

'Yeah. I wasn't sure about it at first, but she seems to have it all planned out. I know we'd agreed to little presents and we've already got her that lovely silk scarf you chose, but I was wondering if we could look at contacting the cruise line and see if we could get her a nice bottle of champagne or something delivered to her cabin as a bit of a surprise.'

As their eyes met across the worktop, Laurie felt such a surge of love for Jake it quite took her breath away. He'd come so far in repairing the relationship with his mum, a lot further than Laurie had expected, and she was delighted at the thoughtfulness of the idea. 'I think it's brilliant. Tell her to send us all her booking details so we have them in case of an emergency and then I'll try and find a number for their customer services.'

'Sneaky.' Jake grinned. 'I'll make an undercover journalist of you yet.'

She laughed. 'I'll leave that to the professionals. Speaking of which, did you get your article submitted?' He'd been nose deep in his laptop with his headphones on when she'd left their cottage that morning, so she hadn't wanted to disturb him for more than a quick kiss goodbye.

'Yeah. I hope I didn't wake you when I got up.'

Laurie shook her head. She'd felt him slide out from beside her, but used to the odd hours he worked by now, she'd rolled into the warm bit he'd vacated and gone straight back to sleep. 'I hope you won't be too tired to go out tonight though.' They were meeting up with her brother, Nick, and a few friends for a drink in the pub to kick off the holiday festivities.

Jake checked his watch. 'Once I've finished helping you with this, I might shoot home and get my head down for a couple of hours. Unless you need me to stick around?'

'No, I'll be fine. I don't suppose it'll be very busy, and I can always give Mum a shout if I have a sudden rush.' The weather might have improved, but people were busy with their last minute preparations and were more likely to pop in for a take-away coffee in passing than want to sit and linger. They finished off the rest of the orders in companionable silence, the only sound in the kitchen the endless round of Christmas hits playing on the radio. 'That's that then,' Laurie said with a sigh of relief as she pushed the last box across the table towards Jake. 'Thanks for helping out.'

Jake secured the order form to the top of the box and set it on the neat stack he'd made. 'Spending time with you is never a hardship, you know that.' He tucked his hands in the front pocket of his jeans. 'Right, unless you've got anything else you need me to do, I'm going to head home.'

Laurie planted her hands on her hips. 'Haven't you forgotten something?' She'd meant it as a tease to imply he'd forgotten to give her a goodbye kiss but at the shadowed look in his eyes she realised there was something else. 'Jake?'

With a sigh, he backed up against the counter and crossed his feet at the ankles. 'Mum wants to give us money for a deposit if we want to buy a place of her own.'

'That's wonderful!' As soon as she'd uttered the words, Laurie wished them back because it was clear Jake was conflicted about it. 'I mean, it's very generous of her to make the offer...' She let the words trail off, not sure what her next step should be in what was rapidly becoming a conversational minefield. 'Talk to me?'

Folding his arms across his chest, Jake stared down at his boot-clad feet for a long moment. 'I know I should be grateful, and I know it would make things a lot easier for us...'

Sensing his hesitation, Laurie planted her feet on either side of his legs and placed her hands on his shoulders. 'We don't need it. I already have my savings.' She and Nick had been putting away as much as they could afford with the intent of repaying their parents for the years of free room and board since they'd started working. Her parents had point-blank refused to accept it, so they had somewhere close to £20,000 in a joint account to share between them.

'I've got a bit set aside as well, but if we took Mum up on her offer, we'd have a nice cushion. It would also give us more options as to the kind of property we might look at.' Jake leaned forward to rest his forehead against hers.

She could almost hear the internal battle he was having with himself. They'd talked a bit about buying rather than renting. It made more sense to spend money on an investment for their future rather than putting it in someone else's pocket. Laurie adored their little cottage perched on the top of the Point in the grounds of the Walker's farm, and in an ideal world they would try and buy it, but she didn't think they'd be willing to sell off the lucrative holiday let. 'We're not in any hurry.'

'It's not that.'

When he didn't say anything else Laurie swallowed a smile. It wasn't that she found the situation amusing, more that she was going to have to confront him head on to get him to say what was really bothering him. 'It's because the money comes from your dad.'

Jake's arms closed round her. 'Stupid, isn't it?' he muttered against her ear. 'You'd think I'd be happy to take it, it's not like he doesn't owe me.'

Laurie leaned back in his hold so she could raise her hands to cup his face, wanting him to read the sincerity of her next words in her gaze. 'If you were the kind of man who thought like that, you wouldn't be the one I'm so madly in love with.'

That earned her a smile. 'Madly, is it?'

'Hopelessly.' She kissed the curve of his mouth. 'Overwhelmingly.' Another kiss and she felt his smile widen beneath her lips. 'Wholeheartedly. Undisputedly. I am eternally and madly in love with you.' She peppered each declaration with a press of her lips to his until he swept her up against him and she had no more breath for words.

'Here's a thought,' Laurie said a few minutes later as she leaned against the warm, lean strength of his body. 'What if we took the money and used it as an investment?'

'Stick it in a savings account, you mean? I don't think interest rates are high enough to make it worth our while. Not without locking it away for years, and then what's the point?'

Laurie tipped her face up so she could look at him properly. 'We're happy as we are right now, yes?'

Jake nodded. 'For sure.' A questioning frown creased his brow. 'Aren't we?'

Laurie laughed. 'Yes! Stop trying to read a deeper meaning into everything. The investment I have in mind is Nick's development project.'

'The warehouse conversion?' The family on Laurie's mother's side owned a warehouse on the dock which they'd used as a storage and processing plant when they'd operated a deep-sea trawler. Since their uncle had switched his business to providing boat trips for tourists and nature enthusiasts, the warehouse had sat empty. Nick wanted to convert it into four apartments, including one for himself, with a plan to sell the other three to locals who like many of their generation were struggling to find homes in the Point.

She nodded. 'I've already told him his half of the savings account is there when he needs it, but what if we could give him more? I'd be happy to loan him my half as well – and, if you think it's a good idea, we could add on the money your mum wants to give us. Better it's us that profit from the eventual sale than the bank clawing it back in interest.'

'That's certainly an idea.' She watched as he thought about it for a minute, and she could almost see the calculations going on inside his head. 'If we get behind him, he's more likely to get the rest of the funding he needs.'

'Yes.' She tried not to sound too hopeful. Nick was already in two minds about whether he had a future in the Point, and though he never said anything about it, she thought he was still caught up in his feelings for Aurora Storm. The pop star had sneaked into the village to film some publicity stunts and had recruited Nick to help her. She'd left the Point just as stealthily as she'd arrived, taking a fair chunk of Nick's heart along with her. Laurie's own feelings about the woman were less than charitable. The Point might have benefited from the influx of interest Aurora had generated, when she'd staged a series of mermaid sightings as part of a viral publicity campaign for her comeback album, but the cost to Nick had been too high. If she and Jake were able to show him how much they believed in him, maybe he'd start believing in himself again.

'It would mean staying in the cottage for another couple of years, assuming the Walker's will let us continue to rent it long term,' Jake said, drawing her away from thoughts of the woman who'd broken her brother's heart.

'I know we've talked about buying a place together, but there's no desperate rush because our circumstances aren't going to change anytime soon. If we can make a decent return on the flats, that would put us in an even better position to buy somewhere.'

Jake leaned down and pressed his nose to hers. 'Listen to us, being all serious, and grown up about stuff. Next thing you know we'll be talking about marriage and babies.'

There was a twinkle in his eye, but she thought she caught the flash of something behind it. *Tread carefully, Laurie.* She pressed a soft kiss against his jaw and kept her voice light as she said: 'Only if you really want to.'

His arms tightened round her. 'Can I register a firm yes to the first and a neutral on the second?' Laurie's heart began to race as the significance of his words hit home. She had always assumed she'd have a family of her own, but it was an expectation rather than a deep and burning desire. She adored her family, had been blessed with parents who cherished and protected her, and she knew any children she might choose to have would be equally well loved. But Jake hadn't had that same experience, so was it really a surprise if he didn't feel the same way?

She stepped back so she could see his face properly but kept her hands locked on his waist so he would know she wasn't pulling away from him. 'You don't have to pretend you might want children because you think that's what I want to hear.' His face was shuttered, eyes blank, mouth compressed into a flat line. For a moment it was like staring at the old Jake, the one who kept everything locked inside. Though her heart ached at the thought he was retreating from her, she held her peace and hoped with enough time he would find what he needed to say.

'I never entertained the possibility of it,' he admitted at last. 'But then again I never entertained the possibility of someone like you coming into my life. Letting myself love and be loved by you is already more than I thought I could handle.' He fell silent again for a long moment. 'Would it be a deal-breaker for you?'

It was her turn to stay quiet, because this was the first time she'd confronted the possibility of a life without children. She thought about what she had, the future she was building for herself – for them – in terms of her business and wondered where, if anywhere, children would fit into that. Would the potential of raising a family with someone else be more fulfilling than continuing to explore the wonderful experience of being with Jake? She didn't know, but she also didn't want to go back to what her life had been before he'd walked into her café. 'I love you. I love us. I want this. I might feel differently about it later, but now, in this moment, I have everything I need to be happy.'

'I want this too, and I meant what I said about being neutral on the topic of kids. If I was dead set against it, I'd say so, whatever it might cost me. I'd never lie to you about something as important as that, not even by omission.' Jake stroked a gentle hand through her hair, wrapping the ends of it round his fist as though unconsciously needing to hold onto her. 'We have time yet, don't we?'

Laurie nodded, giving him what she hoped would be a reassuring smile. 'My biological clock isn't even thinking about ticking.' She closed the small distance between them and nestled against his chest, showing him that he had her, that she wasn't going anywhere. 'I think we should agree to both actively consider how we feel about it and come back to it at a later date.'

He pressed a kiss to the top of her head. 'Okay, but the marriage thing is non-negotiable.'

She laughed. 'Is that your idea of a proposal?'

Jake loosened one arm from behind her back and touched her chin. When she looked up, there was a determination in his eyes. 'It's a statement of intent. I'll do whatever it takes for us to both live our best lives and I want more than anything for that to mean we do it together. Maybe I'll have a chat with Dr Tom in the new year, and see what he recommends in terms of counselling. If I let all this shit with my dad mess up the best thing that's ever happened to me, I'll never forgive myself. I don't want to not have kids because of how my father made me feel growing up, but I also don't want to have them because I have a point to prove about being a better man than him, or because it's the only way I can keep us together. I owe that to myself; I owe it to us.'

Stretching on her toes, Laurie kissed him with all the love in her heart. 'You are already a better man than him. You don't owe me anything other than your love, Jake. Everything else?' She shook her head, because she didn't have the answer any more than he did. 'All we can do is keep on talking, keep on listening and just do the best we can.'

5

ALEX

This is Leicester Square. Change here for the Northern line.
This is a Piccadilly line service to Rayners Lane.

Alex breathed a sigh of relief as the heaving train came to a stop and his fellow passengers pushed and jostled each other as they tried to be first out of the door. A slow trickle of sweat crept down his spine beneath the blue and white striped shirt he had foolishly layered beneath a navy jumper, and a black moleskin blazer over his best black jeans. In a fit of what can only be called madness, he'd added his black wool winter overcoat before leaving the house an hour earlier. He'd been fine on the bitterly cold fifteen-minute walk to his local tube station, but the descent to the platform had felt like a trip down into the bowels of hell between the multitudes of Christmas shoppers crowding the escalators and the infernal heat trapped in the deep tunnels of the Piccadilly line. He'd started to overheat within seconds of the doors closing on the carriage, but crammed in like a sardine in the corner he'd had barely enough room to loosen the scarf round his neck and unbutton his coat. Even that little bit of movement had brought a muttered imprecation from a woman he'd accidentally jostled. Though he'd positioned himself close to the door, it was impossible to break into the stream of disembarking passengers without risking a major incident, so he held his spot and waited for his turn. He wasn't exactly in a hurry to make the meeting his editor, Imogen, had insisted upon. Oh, she'd dressed it up in a pretty bow by saying it was a Christmas drink to celebrate the success of the past year, but they both knew there was only one thing on Immy's mind and that was when Alex was going to turn in the draft of his next book.

Distracted by the impending awkwardness of that conversation, Alex missed his chance, and the people waiting on the platform began to pour into the carriage. He didn't like to use his size, but if he didn't act quickly he'd be hemmed in again and halfway to Covent Garden. That wouldn't be the end of the world, but he hated the bloody lifts there. Squaring his shoulders he stepped into the doorway, blocking a couple of women who'd had a very successful shopping trip given the number of bags they each carried. 'Sorry,' he said, flashing his most winning smile at them as he forced them to stop in their tracks. Their scowls turned quickly to smiles as they took him in. The brunette went so far as to take a step back to make room for him to exit, and receiving a curse for her troubles from someone behind her. With a few more smiles and apologies, Alex shouldered his way free of the pack swarming the platform and fell into step with the stream of people heading for the escalators.

When he emerged onto Charing Cross Road, the traffic was bumper to bumper. Impatient pedestrians wove their way between buses, cars and taxis as they crossed from one crowded pavement to the other. Finding a quiet spot against the wall, he quickly stripped off his coat and jacket and hooked them over one arm. The wind whipped round him, sending a few bits of rubbish dancing in a mini whirlwind down the street, but he welcomed the sudden chill after the stifling heat on the Underground. Hoping to avoid the worst of the crowds, Alex turned into Cranbourn Street and began making his way towards The Ivy where Immy had reserved them a table for lunch. Thinking about the upmarket bar and restaurant conjured the image of a pretty, red-headed woman of the same name and he found himself wondering what she was up to. Would she be bent over her sewing machine beavering away on some last minute present? Perhaps she was sitting in Laurie's café enjoying a steaming mug of hot chocolate and a slice of some decadent treat. *Places I'd rather be...* Alex shook the thought away. He would leave the romance to his brother Tom and worry about more important things – like his looming deadline for starters.

On arrival, he handed his coat in and was about to shrug back into his jacket when the young woman managing the cloakroom offered to take it for him as well. 'If you're sitting in the Central Dining Bar you don't need your jacket,' she said with a smile.

'Thanks,' he said with some relief. 'It's hard to know how many layers you need on days like this.'

Having given Immy's name, he was escorted by a waiter into the old-fashioned glamour of the bar. A wave of noise hit him as they entered the busy room. Almost every seat was filled, from the low-backed stools circling the iconic oval bar, to the tables lining the banquettes. The server led him to a table by the far wall where his editor was waiting for him, her eyes glued to the phone in her hand as she tapped away. 'Thank you,' Alex said to the waiter, causing Immy to glance up from her phone.

'Alex! Oh, how wonderful to see you.' Standing and edging her slight frame between the tables she stretched on tiptoe to peck a kiss to his cheek.

'I'll be back in a moment with your menus,' the waiter said before turning away to answer a hail from another table.

'Sit, sit!' Immy's words spilled out in a flurry as she flapped a hand towards the chair with its back to the room and resumed her seat against the wall. 'I thought you'd be better in that rather than squeezing in here.'

She made it sound like he was a giant, which compared to her petite five-feet-two he supposed he was. 'That was thoughtful of you.' Alex took his seat and tried to smile through his dread of the meeting to come.

'You're looking well!' Immy lied.

He knew she was lying because he'd had ample time to regard his reflection as he'd snipped and scraped off the terrible beard he'd been cultivating for the past few months. He looked a bit more presentable, but there'd been nothing he could do about the deep shadows round his eyes and the hint of an extra chin he'd been hiding under the scraggy facial hair. He'd managed to do up his jeans with a deep breath, but his belt was a notch looser than usual. Too much booze and junk food and not enough exercise was beginning to take its toll. He had a large enough frame he could carry the extra pounds, but he didn't like the general lethargy that came with them. 'You're looking great, yourself,' he countered, his own words sincere. 'I like what you've done with your hair.'

Immy raised a hand to the sleek bob framing her face. 'Do you really like it? I fancied a change, and it's so much easier in the mornings. I'd rather have an extra cup of coffee than spend hours faffing around.' She had the kind of pale skin and neat features he thought of as natural beauty, though he had an adept enough eye to see the subtle enhancements just the right amount of make-up could bring.

The waiter returned and handed them both menus before

waiting expectantly for their drinks order. Not bothering to open it, Immy held the menu to her chest and sent Alex a bright grin. 'Let's have some bubbles, shall we?' Not waiting for his response, she turned her smile to the waiter. 'A couple of glasses of house champagne please.' When the waiter had departed once more she set her menu to one side then folded her arms on the table and leaned towards Alex. 'Now then, what have you been up to? Tell me *everything*.'

He was sure Immy wanted to hear about his writing – or not-writing if he was going to be honest with himself about the mess he was in, but the question was general enough he could swerve the inevitable for a few minutes longer. 'My brother relocated to the coast a few months ago so I've been spending a lot of time down there helping him and the kids settle in.'

'Oh, how wonderful. I so miss being close to the sea. I visit my parents when I can, but things have been manic in the office, so I don't get down to Dorset as often as I'd like.' Immy accepted her glass of champagne from the returning waiter, waited until Alex took his and then raised it in a toast. 'Merry Christmas, to the most eligible bachelor on my books.'

Alex all but snorted champagne up his nose as he choked on her words. 'I... err, you're joking, right?'

Immy laughed, a tinkle of sound that was as pretty and delicate as everything about her. 'Oh, come on, Alex. I know we agreed that our in-house team would run the socials for The Heartbreak Kid to help protect your anonymity, but can you honestly tell me you haven't taken even a little peek at them since the book came out?'

He could honestly swear he never had. Expelling all the pain and anger he'd felt over his ex-wife Jo's betrayal onto paper – well onto the screen of his laptop if anyone wanted to get technical about it – had been a cathartic experience. He'd lanced the boil and let the poison seep into the barely fictitious recounting of their entire relationship that had eventually become *The Marriage Rollercoaster* (a title Immy and her publicity team had come up with). Once he'd finished, he'd had no idea what to do with it until Tom had offered to speak to one of the other partners at his surgery who had a sister in the publishing industry. That sister had turned out to be a colleague of Immy's who'd passed on the details of their general submissions' inbox. Alex had submitted his manuscript without much hope of a response. That someone had not only liked his writing enough to agree to publish it, but had liked it enough to offer him a three-book contract had sent Alex's brain into a spin. Without much thought about what he was committing himself to, he'd signed on the dotted line. The following weeks had been a whirlwind of rewrites and edits until by the time he'd had to read his manuscript through for the very final proof check he'd been sick of the sight of it. Immy and her team had shown him the marketing plan and he'd smiled and nodded and thought it sounded like a right load of old rubbish, especially the excruciating moniker they'd come up with. But time had proven he clearly knew as much about book marketing as he did about keeping his wife happy because *The Marriage Rollercoaster* had taken off like a rocket. Deep in the final throes of his divorce, Alex had found little to celebrate about the book's success, though he'd been grateful when he not only earned out his modest advance, but the subsequent royalty payments started arriving.

Realising he'd been quiet too long, he offered Immy an apologetic smile. 'It's not really my thing.' He'd deleted all his personal socials when Jo left him for a co-worker and someone Alex had thought of as friend, unable to cope with the daily memory reminders of the two of them from happier days. She'd been the one who'd documented every step of their relationship, tagging his profile from that first party where they'd met at university. His posts mostly consisted of responses to the annual round of birthday greetings from close friends and random almost-strangers who'd ended up on his friends list. The people he'd wanted to keep in touch with had his phone number and the rest, well he couldn't say he'd thought about them enough to miss them.

Immy laughed. 'Well, I can assure you that the Kid is *very* popular.' She fiddled with her phone for a moment before turning the screen to show him a Twitter account with the cover of his book as the profile picture.

'What am I looking at?'

She rolled her eyes as she thrust the phone close to him. 'Look at the number of followers!'

He frowned at the screen then up at Immy. '45K, as in forty-five *thousand* people?' Surely not.

She lifted one shoulder in a little shrug as she locked her phone and set it back down next to her plate. 'Some of them will be spam accounts, of course, but you have a lot of genuine followers.'

'You mean the Kid does.' He'd told them from the start he wanted nothing to do with it, and he wasn't about to start taking ownership of it now. As much as he'd poured his feelings into the book, it wasn't an autobiography. He'd been in such a vicious mood about Jo he'd exaggerated her actions and smoothed his own until the story he'd told was much less balanced than the reality he'd lived through. And the edits had only punched it up to portray the male lead in the most sympathetic light possible.

'Well, yes of course.' Immy waved his concerns away with a waft of her hand then reached for her champagne. 'Sooooo...' The way she dragged out the word made his stomach lurch. 'Dare I ask how things are going with *Bumper Cars*?'

Alex grabbed up his glass and took a swig to hide a wince at the abbreviated title of his overdue manuscript. During the discussion over a name for the first book, some bright spark had come up with a fairground theme. The follow-up he was supposed to have been working on for the past six months had been provisionally titled *Back in the Bumper Cars: the dating misadventures of The Heartbreak Kid*. When it had been clear that *Rollercoaster* was a hit, marketing had pushed to use the title for the pre-order listing for his next book. Immy had demurred and although they were using the title in-house, the listing had gone up with a holding cover and a generic title. Whether she was a psychic, or more likely just very good at her job, Alex hoped that at least would make things a bit easier as he tried to negotiate his way out of things. Hell bent on putting Jo behind him, Alex had thought the idea of a dating book would be a bit of a laugh and had initially thrown himself into the swing of it. Being paid to go out, get pissed and try and pick up women had seemed like a gift – until he'd actually tried it.

The first night he'd ended up in some poor woman's flat too drunk to be of any use and she'd left him on the sofa to sleep it off. He'd woken in the early hours hung-over, and had crept out to find himself in an unfamiliar part of town. On the taxi ride home it'd been touch and go whether he'd make it without being sick and only hanging his head out the open window like a dog had saved his blushes – and his wallet. It'd been several weeks until he'd been ready to dip his toe back into the water and he had gone out with a group of mates to celebrate a birthday. He'd danced with a couple of nice women and enjoyed himself for the most part – then the sambuca shots had kicked in and he'd ended up hiding in a disgusting stall in the toilets until he could stop crying long enough to say goodbye to the birthday boy and make a run for it. Hoping a less febrile atmosphere would help, he'd allowed several well-meaning friends to fix him up on blind dates. None of which had gone well enough to encourage him to think about a second date. Even worse, he'd made the mistake of exchanging numbers with the last woman and had ended up blocking her after a barrage of late-night texts that veered from friendly to stalkerish with terrifying speed.

And it wasn't as if he hadn't *tried* to write about these experiences. He'd sat at his desk for hour upon hour staring at his screen, willing his fingers to move over the keyboard, for them to type something – anything. But the few paragraphs he'd managed to squeeze out had felt stale and ugly. Now the fury of Jo's betrayal had faded, Alex felt more than a twinge of guilt for indulging his feelings in quite so public a way. Anonymous or not, he'd betrayed her in a manner almost worse than she had him. At least his humiliation had been mostly private. If anyone ever discovered the man behind The Heartbreak Kid, they'd inevitably discover Jo's identity as well. Putting himself back in the spotlight with another book was asking for trouble, especially if his 'other' self was garnering as much online attention as Immy was implying. Now he sat and thought about it, his writer's block made more sense. He hadn't been able to write the follow up book because deep down he didn't *want* to write it. Reaching for his glass, he drained the last of the contents before setting it aside and looking Immy squarely in the eye. 'It's not going. There's no book. I can't write it.'

Her eyes widened a fraction before her mask of professionalism settled back into place. 'Oh, I'm sure it's not that bad.' Reaching out she patted the back of his hand in what he was sure was supposed to be a supportive gesture but to Alex felt as forced and patronising as her smile. 'Every writer has a few doubts, especially when they've been so successful with their debut. You just have to try and set them aside and push through it.'

Alex tried again to explain. 'It just doesn't feel right.'

'Let's order and then you can tell me exactly what you mean.' Immy cut him off with a gesture to the waiter who was hovering at a discreet distance. Alex hadn't even opened his menu and found himself saying he'd have the same as Immy when she ordered shepherd's pie. 'More champagne?' she offered.

He shook his head then looked at the waiter. 'Can I get a bottle of lager, please?'

'Of course, sir.' The waiter smiled back at Immy. 'Champagne for you, madam?'

'Well, it is Christmas.' She gave that tinkling laugh. It was fascinating watching her operate, the way she used her seeming delicateness to charm and disarm. Anyone foolish enough to take her at face value was in for a surprise, as he'd soon found out for himself. She was a stunning combination of sweet smiles and ruthlessness, like a ballerina turned assassin. 'But you must bring me an enormous glass of water as well or I'll never get anything done this afternoon.' The waiter laughed along with her as he gathered their menus, not sparing Alex so much as a glance as he hurried off to do her bidding. Alex watched her expression change as the waiter departed, the dialling down of her smile, the slightest squaring of her shoulders. He braced himself for what was to come. 'Speaking of Christmas,' Immy said, turning once more to face Alex. 'Do you have any plans this year?'

Taken off guard by her unexpected change of tack, Alex found himself waxing lyrical about Mermaids Point and his plan to drive down with his parents to spend a fortnight with his brother, Tom, his niece and nephew and Tom's wonderful new girlfriend, Nerissa. 'She was the housekeeper when Tom took over the surgery there and well, one thing led to another.' Alex paused when the waiter returned with their drinks and cleared away the empty glasses. 'I'm so glad he and Nerissa found each other. He deserves to be happy again.'

'It sounds utterly romantic,' Immy replied. 'Like fate brought them together.' She laughed. 'Listen to me, turning everything into a book plot!'

'It's certainly a happy ending for both of them,' Alex said with a wistful smile. 'They're absolutely mad for each other – it's all a bit sickening, really.' He said it in a way Immy would know he meant the opposite. He was delighted for Tom, and if he was a tiny bit jealous of his brother's good fortune, he'd never breathe a word of it. Not that he was in the market for another serious relationship – once bitten and all that. Then again, he'd tried the casual thing and that had been bloody awful, too. He really was stuck between a rock and a hard place.

'Have you been seeing anyone?' Immy's question was tentative, her tone much softer than her usual bright and breezy manner.

Ivy's image popped into his head for the second time that day, followed swiftly by an echo of the gut-deep reaction he'd had to her. He might not believe in love at first sight, but he'd been drawn to Ivy Fisher in a way he hadn't been to any woman, not even the one he'd married. He'd been so taken with her, the first words from his lips had been like something out of a cornball movie. Thankfully, Nerissa had saved him from himself and shooed him from the room before he'd been able to embarrass himself further. There were many reasons he loved going to visit his brother in Mermaids Point – pretty Ivy was not going to become one of them, however. Even if he was in any kind of frame of mind to ask her out, he didn't want anything to taint the little haven of peace he'd found in Tom's new home. He enjoyed his visits there too much to risk any complications. Besides, Ivy deserved better than him. Hell, every woman deserved better than him until he could get a proper grip.

He picked at the label on his beer bottle, not wanting to read the sympathy, or even worse, pity, he feared he'd see if he looked directly at Immy. 'A couple of dates, nothing to write home about.'

'Or write a book about?'

Alex huffed a half-laugh. 'What gave it away?'

Immy reached for her phone, pressed a few keys and the phone in Alex's shirt pocket immediately started ringing, making him jump in surprise. She cut the call off then laid her phone back down on the table. 'What was that all about?' he asked, not getting her point.

'Just checking it was working.' She stared at him for a long moment before rolling her eyes and reaching for her glass. 'Oh, Alex, why on earth didn't you talk to me about this sooner? If I'd known you were struggling, I could've helped you.' She made it sound so easy, like picking up the phone and confessing abject failure was no big deal.

'I guess I wasn't ready to admit it to myself until it was too late.' He caught himself fiddling with the label on his bottle again and forced himself to set it aside. 'I've let you down.'

Immy shook her head. 'I've let *you* down. I haven't paid attention, or properly considered the emotional impact *Rollercoaster* must have had on you. And I don't mean writing it, I mean going through it all in the first place. It's a very brave book, Alex, and I can understand why you might not want to put yourself in such a vulnerable position again.'

For a stupid moment he thought he might cry. All this time he'd been worrying himself sick when he should have known Immy would understand. She'd been nothing but kind to him throughout the whole experience. Even when she'd pushed him hard during the edits to sculpt his stream of consciousness into a properly crafted book, she'd been careful to balance any criticism with equal amounts of praise. 'I'm an idiot.'

She laughed. 'I'll drink to that!' Raising her champagne, she held the glass towards him and he gave his own sheepish laugh as he clinked his beer against it. 'Now get your notebook out and we'll have a ten-minute brainstorming session to see if we can come up with some ideas to get you past your mental block. After that, I suggest we enjoy the rest of our lunch and forget about everything until the new year.'

Alex almost choked on his beer. 'You can't be serious?'

Immy folded her arms on the table and leaned towards him. 'I'm absolutely serious. Even if inspiration strikes after our chat, you need to let ideas percolate a bit. Take that time off and really enjoy the plans you've got with your family. Giving yourself permission *not* to write for a while is much better than trying to struggle on as you have been.'

'What about my deadline?' He was never going to hit in a million years, but taking more time out felt counter-intuitive.

She waved it away with an airy smile. 'Publication dates get pushed all the time for lots of different reasons.' Expression growing serious, she rested her folded arms on the table and looked him in the eye. 'It would break my heart to let you go, because I think you've found what you are supposed to do, whether or not you believe that. You are a talented writer, Alex, with an appealing voice that readers have really connected with. I meant what I said about taking the pressure completely off yourself for the next couple of weeks. Enjoy your time with your family. I'm back in the office on the 4th of January but it's always chaotic the first few days after a break so we'll put something in the diary for the week after. We'll brainstorm a few ideas now and then you can take that first week of January to sketch things out a bit and then we'll try and crack a working outline between us.'

She reached across and placed a hand on his arm. 'We'll find a way through this. You're not on your own, Alex.'

* * *

Once they'd started tossing ideas around, Alex had managed to fill up several pages of his notebook with scribbled bits and pieces of thoughts he hoped he could develop into something. Feeling much lighter in himself, apart from a rather full stomach, he bade Immy a fond farewell then spent the next couple of hours wandering round Covent Garden. He took a few snaps of the Christmas lights to show Tom's kids and picked up some last minute gifts from the artisan boutiques that lined the glass-roofed market, his brain playing around with some of the things he and Immy had come up with all the while.

If anyone had asked him, he would've said he'd rather stick pins in his eyes than be wandering the crowded shopping area this close to Christmas, but there was such a lovely atmosphere he found himself exchanging smiles and friendly apologies with the people he inevitably bumped into. Groups of friends were huddled beneath space heaters outside pubs while parents herded their excited children towards the bright lights of Leicester Square to find something to eat before joining the queue for whatever West End show they planned to see. He'd been making his way back to the tube when a comment from a passing couple about something on Twitter had sparked another idea. He'd ended up side-tracking into a pub where he'd secured a tiny table in the corner and spent the next forty minutes scrolling through the myriad of comments beneath the posts his alter-ego had supposedly written, and scribbling notes as he downed another couple of beers. Happy that he had the bones of something to work upon, Alex chucked his notebook into the top of one of his shopping bags, and wandered along in a little bubble of renewed hope as he made his way back towards the tube station. The train ride home was even more cramped than the one into town, but he didn't care. He felt free for the first time in months, out from under the weight of his own and other's expectations, no longer shackled by the crippling sense of failure which had burdened him for months.

The sense of peace lasted until he turned into the gate of the red-bricked terrace that hadn't felt like home for far too long. He stopped dead at the sight of the small blonde figure of his ex-wife perched on the front steps in the oversized Parka he'd purchased for her their first winter together, frustrated at her lack of practical clothing. He couldn't remember the last time he'd seen her wear it. It certainly didn't suit the sleek style she'd adopted once they'd left university and started inching their way up the corporate ladder. Her legs were clad in sheer black tights and heels far too high for the treacherous state of the pavements now the sun had set and the temperature had dropped below freezing. She was also clutching a bottle of wine, which didn't bode well for her mood.

'What are you doing here, Jo?' He hated the hostility in his tone the moment he heard it. Not because he didn't feel hostile towards the woman who'd shattered his dreams of happiness and undermined the confidence which had been the rock on which he'd built his self-esteem. He might still be hurting, but damn it, she didn't need to know that.

She waved the bottle of wine towards the door in a belligerent gesture. 'You changed the locks, so I had no choice but to wait out here in the freezing cold.' Her pretty face with its wide blue eyes and slightly pointed chin was a picture of surprise and outrage that he would do such a thing.

Swallowing down a flash of temper that she'd had the

audacity to even try and enter the house after walking out eighteen months previously, he dumped his shopping bags on the step and fished round in his pocket for his key. It took him several attempts to unlock the door, his hands were shaking that much. *It's just the cold, nothing more.* 'You don't live here, remember?' he snapped, as he finally got the key to turn and shoved open the door.

When he glanced down it was to find Jo holding up a pink hoodie decorated with sparkly silver moons and stars he'd spotted in a window display and thought Emily would love. 'Put that down!' Snatching it from her hands, he shoved it into the top of the bag. The rough gesture tipped over the rest of his shopping, sending the contents spilling out. 'Christ!'

Irritated that he was letting her mess with his good mood, Alex took a deep breath as he tossed the bag he was holding into the hall before bending over to gather his scattered belongings. Jo decided to stand up at that moment, even though he was half-leaning over her, and the top of her head would've connected with his chin if he hadn't taken a hasty step back. He caught her open bottle of wine with his heel, knocking it over the edge of the steps in the process. The acid-grape scent of cheap white wine filled the air. At least the bottle had survived its fall into the flower bed so he wouldn't be faced with trying to pick up bits of broken glass in the morning.

Ignoring the wine, Jo was trying to stuff the shopping back into the bags, her unsteady hands doing little more than creasing everything. It was like something out of a farce, and might even have been amusing if he wasn't caught up in the middle of it. 'Leave it,' Alex said, wishing she would just leave, full stop. 'I'll sort it out in a minute.'

'I'm only trying to help.' It was said in a voice he hated, the one that said he was being unreasonable. Funny how *he'd* always been the unreasonable one in their marriage. Bloody hilarious, in fact.

Realising he'd left the door wide open he had no choice but to let her take hold of the bags while he edged his way round her in order to block the threshold. 'What are you doing here, Jo?'

She handed him the shopping bags in a grand gesture, like she'd done him some huge favour. Not bothering to look inside, he slung them behind him to join the other one then braced his hands on either side of the door frame, barring any attempt she might think about making to step inside.

'Season of Goodwill to all Men and all that jazz.' The hand she waved in a dismissive gesture spoke of a breezy confidence, but the edges of her smile had started to wilt in the face of his flat gaze.

'I asked you a question.'

Jo cast a quick glance over her shoulder, but the street was dark and still, the neighbours all safely ensconced behind their fairy-light festooned windows and doors. 'Can't we talk about this inside? It's freezing out here.'

Alex maintained his solid stance, refusing to acknowledge the rush of heat escaping from the open door behind him. 'If you want someone to talk to, I suggest you go home and talk to Shaun. I thought he was *such a good listener*,' he parroted the words she'd flung in his face during their cataclysmic row when she'd tried to justify her betrayal.

'Oh, shut up,' she snapped, the mask of sweetness slipping to betray the selfish, spoilt brat he'd been blinded to until it was far too late.

Alex contemplated just stepping back and shutting the door in her face, but then he pictured the scene she was more than capable of causing and took a reluctant step to the side. 'You've got five minutes.'

Flashing him a sweet smile that made his back molars clench, Jo slipped past him, her body brushing deliberately against him like a cat trying to scent mark her territory – if cats wore perfume that is. Shutting the door, Alex rested his palm against the wood for a long moment as he tried to settle his stomach against the barrage of memories the swirling cloud of *Curious by Britney Spears* conjured in his brain. He only knew the name of it because he'd been the one to buy it for her. He'd gone into Boots the first Christmas they were together and stared in desperate confusion at the long rows of pretty bottles and fancy packaging. When his eyes had finally settled on a display image of the famous pop star he'd felt a surge of relief and grabbed the stylish black and pink box off the shelf like he'd found a prize. Jo had adored the scent and had worn it throughout their relationship – and beyond, it seemed.

Only when he could think past the ghosts in his head did he turn round and brace his back against the closed door. 'Four minutes.'

Ignoring his countdown, Jo unzipped her Parka and let it slide to the floor, revealing a black sequined party dress with a plunging neckline. If she was trying to impress him she was going about it all the wrong way. He'd never liked this over-styled version of her – all smoky eyes and ruby-red lipstick and an edge of hardness. He'd always preferred the softer version, the one she showed very few people – the messy hair and unmade face of Sunday morning strolls to fetch the papers and eat sticky pastries in their local café. She looked round the hall. 'You haven't changed much about the place.'

What was he supposed to say to that? If she thought he'd kept everything the way it was because he'd created some sort of shrine to her memory then she was in for a disappointment. He'd not changed anything because he hadn't cared enough about anything other than his rage over her betrayal to think once, never mind twice about redecorating. The paint wasn't peeling, the sofa and his bed were comfortable, the fridge and other appliances worked and that was all that had mattered. It wasn't like he couldn't afford to do it – the money from *Rollercoaster* had built his bank balance up to a very healthy level – he just wasn't bothered.

He looked at her now and waited for the bitterness and fury to rise... He waited. And waited. Yes, he was irritated after all the faffing round on the doorstep just now, and no, he didn't want to be having to deal with her when he'd planned to flop on the sofa with a beer and a sandwich while he watched a movie. But that awful, ugly hatred he'd wallowed in was missing. Maybe he was still too numb with relief from his meeting with Immy to feel anything else, but he didn't think so.

Taking his time he studied the woman before him. Objectively she was still as appealing as when he'd first laid eyes on her. Hair the shade of ripened wheat twisted into one of those deceptively casual styles that he knew from lying on the bed watching her at her dressing table took ages to achieve. Elegant swan neck leading to slim shoulders with a hint of collarbone showing in the neckline of her dress. Breasts he knew the shape and weight of like a muscle memory, the same way he knew the dip of her waist, the curve of her hips and every inch of the slender legs clad in sheer black tights that would feel like silk beneath his hands should he stroke them. But there was no itch in his fingers to touch her, no thrum of anticipation, none of the heat that had always coursed through his veins for her. He felt... nothing. Like an empty hearth dusted with the ash of a long-burnt out fire. 'You look like you're all dressed up and ready to go,' he said, more for something to fill the silence than out of any real interest.

'It's the office Christmas party, tonight. The guys stayed in work but most of the ladies went home to get changed.' She held out her hands as though inviting him to praise her outfit.

He knew the routine – after all, they'd worked together at the same big five accountancy firm until her infidelity had come to light. 'You always did enjoy an office party. You had a particular fondness for the copier cupboard, I recall.' He felt a sharp bite of satisfaction as he watched a flush mottle her throat and cheeks. It had been a cheap shot, perhaps, but even his new mellowed out attitude towards her had limits. Deciding he'd had more than enough of this trip down memory lane, he pushed away from the door and reached for the latch. 'Don't let me keep you.'

'You could if you wanted.' Her voice was husky, and when he glanced over his shoulder at her she'd struck a pose – that was the only word he could think of to describe it – one hand on her hip, the other resting on the post at the foot of the stairs as though she might invite him to follow her up at any moment.

It was an audacious enough move he was almost willing to give her credit for it. Almost. 'What about Shaun?' There was no way in hell he was going to take her up on the offer, but he was curious enough to want to know what was going on in her head.

'Forget about him.' She took a step towards him, her tongue flashing over her scarlet-red lower lip in a calculated invitation. 'I don't want to think about anything other than us.'

If she'd said she and Shaun had broken up would he have felt something other than the disgust and disappointment spreading through his gut? Perhaps, though nothing like the desire she'd obviously come here hoping to stir in him once more. Had she said the same thing to his former friend when she'd first tried to seduce him? Though he held them equally responsible for what had happened, Shaun had told him Jo had been the one to make the first move which had destroyed their marriage. He pondered idly for a moment, wondering what

Shaun had done to send her scuttling back to him before he dismissed it. It didn't matter why she was here, only that he wanted her gone. 'There is no us.'

He watched his words register, watched her wobble just a touch on her too-high heels before she caught herself and straightened up. The seductive smile fell away, her bright red lips twisting into an ugly scowl as she folded her arms across her chest. 'Is there someone else? Is that who you bought that bargain-basement hoodie for?' she asked, voice dripping with jealousy.

As though his subconscious had been waiting for an excuse, Alex thought not of his niece, the intended recipient of the gift, but of Ivy the first time he'd seen her at Tom's back door. Her messy cap of red curls had been blown every which way by the wind and the smattering of freckles across her pale cheeks hadn't been hidden under a caked-on layer of thick foundation. Her Wellington boots had been the same red as Jo's lipstick, her legs encased in skinny jeans she'd paired with what had looked like a vintage men's smoking jacket. Unlike Jo who so often dressed to impress others, Ivy had struck him as someone who wore whatever pleased her.

Though he'd sworn off Ivy, it was enough to hold onto the idea of her – the promise of what his attraction to her meant. For the first time since Jo had ripped his heart out, he felt something like hope for the future. 'That's none of your business.'

'So, there is someone?' Jo seemed to perk up a little at that, as though she could only comprehend him not being willing to let her back into his life because he'd replaced her.

He considered making his lack of feelings for her crystal clear, but if the thought of him being with someone else meant he could get rid of Jo quicker then he didn't need the petty satisfaction hurting her would bring. He reached once more for the latch and opened the door, letting in a blast of air with a wintery edge to it. 'Goodbye, Jo.'

She stared for a long moment as though waiting for him to change his mind before scooping her Parka from the floor and shrugging into it. He wondered if she'd chosen it on purpose, a reminder of who they'd once been to each other. She patted the voluminous front pockets of the jacket as though checking for something – her evening bag, probably – then marched to the door, heels clicking on the tiles of the hallway. When she passed him this time she made sure to keep a distance between them.

He went to close the door, but she swung round and pressed a hand against it. 'It didn't have to come to this, you know. I never wanted Shaun, not really, I just wanted you to notice me again.' She pushed against the door, but he held it in place, not willing to concede an inch to her. 'If you'd asked me to come back, I would've dropped everything for you.' A puzzled frown etched a line between her brows. 'Why didn't you ever ask me to come back?'

Alex closed his eyes for a second against a wave of unutterable sadness. She'd destroyed everything they'd had, everything they could've had in the future because she'd wanted more attention? He felt a momentary flash of pity for Shaun before deciding neither of them was worth it. 'The fact you don't understand why just goes to show you never really knew me at all.' And with that he pushed the door gently, but firmly closed.

6

IVY

'Mum?' Ivy followed the quiet question with a tap on the door of what had once been the dining room in their cottage and waited, half-hoping her mum had managed to drop off to sleep.

'Come in, darling.' As she entered the shadowed room she saw her mum was already struggling to sit up straighter, and Ivy hurried over to help rearrange and fluff the pillows. 'That's better,' Jennifer Fisher said as she rested her head back. 'Here now let me look at you.'

Trying to ignore the hint of breathlessness in her mother's voice, Ivy held out her arms and turned in a slow circle to show off the outfit she'd chosen for the evening. 'What do you think?'

'You look pretty as a picture. I thought when you brought that dress home it was the perfect shade of green.'

Ivy laughed. 'And here's me remembering you saying it looked like an old sack of nothing.'

Jen lifted a finger and wagged it at her. 'And I wasn't wrong, but I always had faith in your skills as a seamstress. Apart from the colour, it's barely recognisable.'

Ivy brushed a hand over the velvety material which had drawn her eye in a local charity shop a couple of months ago and allowed herself a little smile of pride. The vintage 80's party dress had been unstitched, trimmed and reshaped into a fitted knee-length tunic. Gone were the puffball shoulders, replaced by long sleeves that ended in a point which partly covered the backs of her hands. She'd added iridescent beads, reclaimed from a moth-eaten handbag, to the tips of the points, and round the high collar of the tunic. The dress had cost her a fiver, and the ladies in the charity shop had thrown the bag in for free because Ivy was one of their most loyal customers. 'I am rather pleased with the way it turned out.'

'So you should be.' Her mum patted the side of the bed next to her. 'Now come and tell me all about your plans for the evening.'

'It's nothing special,' Ivy said as she picked up her mum's hand and traced her fingers over the paper-thin skin. 'Just a pre-Christmas drink with Laurie and a few others.' After several years of not speaking, Ivy and her former best friend had recently taken tentative steps to rebuild their friendship. It was too early to say whether they'd ever get back to anything like their former closeness, but Ivy was just grateful to be back on speaking terms.

'Nice of her to invite you,' Jen said, echoing Ivy's own thoughts. 'It gives me such peace of mind to know you'll have a friend like her around in the months to come.'

'Don't Mum.' Ivy closed her eyes, all the joy she'd been feeling about the prospect of doing something normal for a couple of hours seeping away.

Her mother flipped their hands so she was the one doing the petting. 'We have to talk about it, darling.' When Ivy kept her eyes closed, her mum shook her hand gently. 'I had a long chat with Dr Tom earlier and we've got it all settled.'

Ivy's lids flew open at that. 'Got *what* settled?'

Her mum's smile was the same as she remembered it from when she'd been a little girl. For a moment Ivy felt nothing but secure and safe in the bonds of love that bound the two of them together. But there was no denying the lines of pain bracketing her mother's eyes, nor the sunken cheeks where the horrible, creeping disease the name of which Ivy couldn't bring herself to say any more had leached away the flesh and vitality. 'He's found me a place at the hospice, and I'll be moving in there just after new year.'

'No!' Ivy couldn't hold in the cry of protest. 'You're staying here with me, where you belong.'

'It's too much for you, love.' Jen reached out to tuck a curl behind Ivy's ear.

'No. No it isn't.' Ivy bit her lip as she looked away, willing herself not to give in to the tears she could feel burning the backs of her eyes. Nothing was too much when it came to the woman who'd given her everything. It wasn't easy, and she knew it bothered her mum when she had to do things for her that were a reversal of the kind of care she'd needed as a child, but it didn't bother Ivy in the slightest.

'Well, it's too much for me, then. You already have to do practically everything for me and it's only going to get worse.'

'Don't say that,' Ivy whispered as she lowered her head to rest it on her mum's thigh.

Her mum's soft hands stroked through her hair. 'But I have to say it, darling, and you have to accept it. It won't be much longer now, and I won't spend our last few weeks together being a burden on you. I don't want those to be the memories you have to carry of me.'

'You're not a burden,' Ivy choked out. 'I don't want some stranger taking care of you! It's my job to look after you.'

'Hush. Look at me.' Ivy forced herself to sit up, sniffing back the tears which had managed to break free. 'Oh no, no tears,' Jen protested as she reached for the box of tissues resting on the bed covers beside her. 'Wipe your face before you spoil that lovely make up.'

Ivy rose from the bed and took a seat at the dressing table in the corner. Checking her reflection in the mirror she dabbed at the stray streaks of mascara at the corners of her eyes and practised a few of the deep breathing techniques she'd learned from her meditation app. She'd originally downloaded it for her mum so she could listen to the bedtime stories, but in recent months she'd found herself dipping into it more and more as a resource to help centre her own fears and stress. Feeling a bit calmer, she retook her place on the edge of the bed. 'Sorry for being a drama llama.'

Her mum laughed, as Ivy had hoped she would. 'Oh, darling, you might be the least dramatic person I know.' Her face grew serious for a moment. 'And that's one of the things that bothers me most about all... this.' She waved a hand at herself, the gesture encompassing so much of their shared grief and frustration.

'I'm fine, Mum. You don't need to worry about me,' Ivy reassured her.

Jen pursed her lips. 'I'm your mother, of course I'm going to worry about you. Especially when you've put most of your life on hold to look after me.' It was her turn to look away. 'The thing I hate about this bloody monster is that it's consuming you as well as me. It's already robbed you of so much, I can't allow it to steal a moment more of your life.'

'You know I don't feel like that, don't you? I love you, Mum, I'd do anything for you.' Too late Ivy realised the trap she'd laid for herself with those words.

'And that's why you're going to let me do what I think is for the best and not fight me on it any more. I don't have much time left, darling, please let me have autonomy over what happens while I still have enough strength to make these kind of decisions.'

Ivy opened her mouth as she struggled to find the words that would change her mother's mind before reluctantly closing it with a nod. 'If you're sure it's what you want then I respect your decision, Mum.'

'Thank you.' Jen took both Ivy's hands. 'We're going to have a lovely Christmas together, okay? No tears, only laughter, promise me.'

Ivy gave her a watery smile. 'That might be a bit more than I can manage, but I'll try.'

'Good girl. Now give me a kiss and go on out and enjoy yourself. I've already spoken to Sylvia and she's going to pop in later for a chat. She'll see me settled for the night, so I don't want you clock-watching and thinking you need to rush back.'

Just as she and Laurie had been friends since they were little, so her mum and Laurie's mum had been. 'You'll message me, though, if you need me?'

'I'll be fine,' Jen replied with a hint of exasperation.

'*Mum.*' Now it was Ivy's turn to insist because she'd only be able to relax and enjoy herself if she knew her mum wasn't going to suffer unnecessarily just to give her a night off.

'All right, I promise. Give Laurie a kiss from me – and that charming brother of hers too.' There was no mistaking the twinkle in her mother's eye as she said it.

'How many times!' Ivy shook her head, but she was laughing as she did it. Her mum and Sylvia had always harboured a little dream that their daughter and son would fall in love, but the idea of dating Nick Morgan creeped Ivy out. Apart from the fact he'd been with more than his fair share of the Point's all-be-it limited number of eligible women, he was like a brother to her. Oh, he was all kinds of good looking, and boy would life have been easier these past few years if she'd had him at her side to lean on but... no, just no.

'Such a shame.' Jen sighed. 'I'd feel a lot happier if I knew I wasn't leaving you on your own. Speaking of which, I think it's past time you made peace with your dad.'

The exasperated humour Ivy felt at her mum's clumsy match-making efforts was doused as effectively as if she'd had a bucket of cold water chucked over her head. She made to get off the bed, but her mum held her back with the softest of touches to the back of her hand. 'Don't ask this of me,' Ivy pleaded, voice a hoarse whisper. 'I'll do anything else, but not this.'

'Your father can't help being who he is,' Jen said in a gentle voice. 'He's always chosen the easy path in life, and no one challenged him on it. Your nanna didn't think she could have children so when Kevin came along they were so delighted they doted on him to the point of spoiling him. I knew he would cause me nothing but trouble, but the heart wants what the heart wants and mine wanted him from the day I was old enough to start thinking about boys as something other than smelly nuisances.'

Ivy didn't want to smile, but she couldn't help herself. 'They're still mostly smelly nuisances.' Jen laughed which quickly turned into a cough that left her breathless and her hands shaking beneath Ivy's as she helped her take a sip from the glass of water beside her bed. When she rested her head against the pillows and closed her eyes to get her breath back, Ivy made herself busy knowing it would take her mum longer to settle if she fussed round her.

She gathered up a couple of stray tissues and put them in the wicker bin in the corner, then picked up the empty jug from the bedside cabinet and took it out into the kitchen to refill it. As she popped ice cubes from a plastic tray she thought about the last time she'd seen Kevin. That's what she called him in her mind these days. He didn't deserve to be thought of as her father, not when he'd walked out on them ten years ago when her mum had first been diagnosed. He couldn't cope, he'd told them in a flood of tears, couldn't bear to watch his beloved Jen suffer. But he'd somehow thought it was okay for thirteen-year-old Ivy to cope, and to watch. *Bastard*. Her mum might harbour some affection for the man, but Ivy had no such tenderness towards him. She took a deep breath and did what she always did and tucked the bitterness deep inside the little mental box she kept in the corner of her mind for all the things she didn't have time to deal with. One day there would be no more room in that box, but as long as her mum needed her, Ivy would keep folding the bad thoughts up and tucking them away.

Returning to the bedroom, she was pleased to see her mum had her eyes open and a bit of colour had returned to her cheeks. When she held up the jug and received a nod, she poured a little of the cold water into the glass before setting it to one side. Jen took the glass without needing help and enjoyed a couple of sips. 'That feels good, thanks darling.'

'It's no trouble,' Ivy said, because it wasn't. Even after Kevin had left them high and dry she'd never minded picking up the strain of taking care of her mum. It was what you were supposed to do for the people you loved. 'Now, are you sure you don't want me to wait with you until Sylvia arrives?' She'd told Laurie she would meet her at six and it was almost that now, but she would understand if Ivy sent her a message saying she would be a bit late.

'No, love. I want you to go out and have a good time.' Jen

reached for her hand and squeezed it. 'I think you misunderstood me just now. Your dad can get in the sea as far as I'm concerned...' Ivy couldn't help a snort of laughter and Jen paused to give her a wicked grin that was so much like her old self it chased away the shadows that had settled between them. 'It's you I'm concerned about, my lovely girl, and only you. As I said before, your dad is who he is and he's never going to change. I want you to forgive him, but only for your sake. It won't do you any good to keep carrying that resentment around, and if you don't let it go then I'm worried it will fester and taint your feelings towards, not just him, but other men who may come into your life.'

The chances of a man coming into Ivy's life were two – fat chance and no chance at all – but she didn't say that. 'I'll think about it.' Later. For now, it was going in the box along with all the other difficult stuff.

Jen squeezed her hand and it was worth the small concession to see a look of relief pass over her face. 'There's just one more thing before I let you go.'

'*Mum*.' Ivy wasn't sure she could handle anything else.

Jen grinned. 'It's a good thing, I promise. Go over to my dressing table and open my jewellery box.'

Ivy did as she was told, taking a seat once more on the delicate pink satin-topped stool and tugged the heavy wooden box towards her. She'd always been fascinated by it since she was a little girl and her mum had let her lift up the intricately carved lid and play dress up with the treasures inside it. 'What am I looking for?' she asked her mother via her reflection in the mirror.

'Your grandmother's jet beads and earrings should be in the top shelf. I think they'll match your outfit perfectly, don't you?'

Ivy lifted the teardrop earrings carefully from where they nestled against the red velvet lining and held them up. 'I've always loved these.' They'd been the reason she'd wanted to get her ears pierced though her mum had made her wait until she was twelve and even then she'd been far too young to carry off something so sophisticated. 'Are you sure?'

'Absolutely.' Jen's reflected smile was indulgent. 'Jewellery is made to be worn, not locked away in a dusty box and forgotten.'

Ivy's fingers closed round the delicate bead drops in her hand. 'I'll wear something of yours every day and smile as I put it on.' It still felt wrong to make such pledges, but how much worse would it be to hold them inside until it was too late to speak them? She knew she'd done the right thing when she caught her mother's gaze and they shared a smile. Blinking rapidly against another surge of emotion, Ivy took her time putting in the earrings and fastening the matching choker round her neck. They picked up and complimented the beadwork she'd added to the tunic and added a dramatic contrast to her naturally pale skin.

'Show me.' At her mother's request, Ivy twisted round on the stool, raised her chin then turned her head slowly from side to side to display the earrings to their full effect. 'Perfect.' When Ivy stood, Jen waved her back down again. 'Look underneath the shelf.'

Turning back to the box, Ivy lifted out the velvet-lined divider and spotted a folded piece of paper nestling on the collection of bangles, watches and other items that made up her mum's collection. She held it up towards her mum. 'This?'

Jen nodded and patted the bed beside her to show she wanted Ivy to sit back alongside her when she unfolded it. With a touch of trepidation – they'd already ridden a rollercoaster of emotion together and Ivy wasn't sure she'd cope with much more until she'd had time to shore up her defences – she opened out the single sheet. 'It's what you've always dreamed about, darling,' her mum said, softly.

Ivy stared down at the first page of an estate agents set of

particulars and wondered what on earth she was going to say. She
knew the building in the picture that dominated the top section
of the flyer almost as well as she knew the house she had lived in
all her life. 'It's Mr Cavendish's bookshop.' Nothing happened in a
place like Mermaids Point without everyone soon catching wind
of it, and when the owner of the village bookshop had announced
he was ready to retire word had spread like wildfire. Ivy had
heard the gossip, same as everyone else, and had tucked away the
little flutter of excitement she'd felt.

Finding something she could do to bring in money while
being able to stay at home with her mum had been a struggle, but
Ivy had always had a talent for sewing and making her own
clothes, or – as she had with her tunic – buying something cheap
from the charity shop and tailoring it to fit. She enjoyed the medi-
tative concentration it took to sit quietly and sew, and it had been
a creative way to channel her stress. It had also saved them
money when they'd only had her mum's income support – and
the bit of money Kevin put into the bank to pay for Ivy's upkeep –
to live upon. Friends had asked her to help with things like
turning up the hem of their school skirts. As she'd got a bit older,
other people had started coming to her with little mending and
alteration jobs and insisted on paying her. She'd never thought of
it as charity, even if some of the work that had come her way had
been from people who were probably capable of doing it themselves. She was providing a service and she had enough confidence in her skills to understand she deserved to be paid in
return. Over time, she started branching out, rescuing bits of old
furniture which she painted and decorated. The smaller pieces
she'd sold through Sylvia and Andrew's eclectic gift shop on the
seafront, the large ones via word of mouth. Now she was the
village's first port of call when it came to fixing things. From
threadbare teddies missing a button eye to the painstaking

repairs she'd made to the crocheted blanket which meant so much to Dr Tom's children; Ivy never turned down a challenge. What she didn't know how to do, she learnt through research and plain trial and error. The whole operation was run from their tiny box room which she'd turned into a workshop. She'd dreamed of expanding into a bigger space one day, but the implications of being able to do that had always been too heartbreaking to bear.

'It's got a flat upstairs as well which would be perfect for you,' her mum said, bringing Ivy's attention back to the leaflet. 'Once I'm in the hospice there'd be no need to hang onto this place any more.'

Shocked to the core at what she was hearing, Ivy whirled on her mother. 'But this is our home, Mum. You can't think I'd want to put it on the market the moment you're gone!'

'But why not?' Jen circled Ivy's hands with both of hers. 'It's just bricks and mortar, darling. Home is where the heart is, as they say. Why cling to the past when you should be planning for a bright new future for yourself? People are crying out for places like this, especially after Mermaids Point has been put so firmly on the map after the antics of that pop star over the summer. Now would be the perfect time to sell.'

A terrible suspicion settled over Ivy. 'Is this why you're so keen to go into the hospice?' The idea horrified her.

'Call it an added bonus.' Her mother's expression held a stubbornness that Ivy just couldn't bring herself to argue with. 'You don't have to make up your mind straight away. Let's think about it over the next couple of weeks and we can talk about all the pros and cons, okay?'

Ivy folded the flyer and put it in the pocket of her tunic – because what right-thinking woman made clothes for herself without decent-sized pockets? 'Okay.'

'Now give me a kiss and go out and have a lovely evening.

Take lots of photos and then you can show them to me in the morning.'

Ivy wasn't sure how she was supposed to relax and enjoy herself after her mother had blindsided her with so much in one go, but she owed it to her to try. *Fold it up and tuck it away in the box*, she told herself as she pressed her lips to her mum's cool cheek. 'I love you, Mum.'

'I love you too, darling, today, tomorrow and always.'

Ivy smiled at the words which had been her mum's special message to her since she was a baby. 'TTA.' She blew her mum a kiss and went to fetch her coat. She'd never felt less like going out in her life, but she knew it would upset her mum if she didn't. Calling out a final goodbye, she tugged on a pair of thick wool gloves and pulled a matching knitted cap over her short red curls. They had a life of their own at the best of times so the few minutes it would take her to walk down to the seafront to The Sailor's Rest wouldn't leave them squashed. As she put her purse and phone in her coat pocket she paused to check the time and realised she was already late. She shut the door behind her, then tugged off one glove and tapped out a quick message as she began to walk.

Sorry. I'm on my way.

The dancing dots appeared in the corner of the WhatsApp screen and then a reply from Laurie popped up.

See you soon x

Tucking her phone away, Ivy quickly pulled her glove back on to protect her fingers from the bitter nip of the night air. The incessant rain of the past few weeks had passed, much to every-one's relief. But the price for enjoying clear blue skies during the day was a freezing plunge below zero as soon as the sun began to set. Tugging her coat up over the bottom of her chin, Ivy hurried down the quiet street.

The moment she turned the corner onto the seafront there were signs of life. All the businesses lining the street had gone to town with their Christmas decorations, and lights glittered and flashed as far as the eye could see. More lights hung from the wrought iron railings and lamp posts lining the edge of the wall which sheltered the village from the worst of the winter storms. It didn't happen often, but Ivy could remember a couple of occa-sions when the sea had been whipped high enough to swallow the beach and crash against its thick stones. Instead of a tree, the village decorating committee had gathered lobsterpots, buoys, and yards of fishing net to create a giant pyramid-shaped struc-ture. Green lights filled the lobsterpots to represent foliage and the buoys shone in white festoons like giant fairy lights. Ivy paused to take pictures of the 'tree' and several of the shop windows to show her mum before she followed the sounds of music and laughter. Ever enterprising, Pete, the landlord of The Sailor's Rest, had set up several standing tables on the pavement outside the pub with space heaters next to them, and a few hardy souls were enjoying their pre-Christmas celebrations outside. Rather them than her, Ivy thought as she hurried into the pub after a man who held the door open for her with a smile.

Heat and noise hit her like a wall, and she was quickly pulling open her coat with one hand and tugging off her hat with the other as her eyes scanned the busy room. Laurie must've been keeping an eye out for her because she popped up on her feet and waved both hands in the air to catch Ivy's attention.

Exchanging greetings, smiles and apologies as she edged her way across the packed bar, Ivy was relieved to plop down on the bench seat next to her friend. 'Phew, seems like the whole village is out tonight!' she said, wriggling out of her coat and folding it up behind her.

'No kidding. I've been defending this table for the past quarter of an hour. I've already lost one of the chairs I was saving for the boys, so we'll have to squeeze up a bit when they arrive.'

'I'm sorry again for being late, I was settling mum for the evening.'

Something must've have shown in her eyes because Laurie reached out and gave her a quick hug. 'Don't even worry about it.' They hadn't quite got back to the hugging stage, so it took Ivy a little off guard, but she was glad of the contact and squeezed Laurie in return. 'I got us a bottle. I hope that's okay?' Laurie asked as she pulled out a bottle of Pinot Grigio from an ice bucket she'd somehow commandeered from Pete.

'Good idea. Save us fighting to the bar every five minutes.'

Laurie laughed. 'Five minutes? Someone is in need of drink!' She made a show of filling up the empty glass almost full and pushed it into Ivy's hands.

'I am!' Ivy giggled as she sucked in a very unladylike slurp from the top of the glass. 'Oh God, that's good.' She took another mouthful then made herself set it back down before she gulped the lot.

'Like that is it?' Laurie's gentle smile was all sympathy as she half-twisted on the bench to face Ivy. 'I told the boys to come a bit later because I thought you might need a bit of quiet time first.' As well as Laurie's boyfriend, Jake, and her brother, Nick, they were being joined by Alex Nelson, who was visiting his family for Christmas. Ivy had only met the new doctor's brother once, but he'd certainly left an impression with his dark good looks and outrageous flirting.

Ivy scrubbed a knuckle across the tip of her nose willing the sudden prickle of impending tears away. 'Oh please, don't be nice to me or I'll be a sobbing mess all night.'

Reaching out, Laurie gave her arm a sudden pinch – not hard, but it was enough to shock Ivy into surprised laughter and was the perfect antidote to the ever-present cloud of sadness hanging over her. When their eyes met, Laurie shrugged a shoulder. 'I can give you a kick on the shin, too, if that'll help.'

'Nooo, thanks all the same.' Laughing they both reached for their glasses and had another drink. Ivy gazed round the room as she let the warmth and familiarity of the place settle her. With the unpredictable weather, the last of the visitors were long gone from the village and she felt safe and protected. Though she didn't *want* to cry, she knew it wouldn't matter if she did. Everyone here knew how things were with her mum, and they'd let her get on with it without staring or whispering. Knowing that was enough to bolster her and she turned back to Laurie with a sigh. 'Mum's talked to Dr Tom about hospice care.'

Laurie bit her lip as she reached out to place a hand on Ivy's thigh where she'd bent her leg to rest it on the seat between them. 'When?'

'In the new year.' Ivy found herself reaching for Laurie's hand and she gripped it tightly, drawing the strength she needed to continue. 'She wants to make the decision while she still feels able. As much as it is absolutely killing me to even think about it, I don't feel I have a choice other than to agree. Especially when she thinks it's for the best.'

'There's nothing else you can do,' Laurie agreed. 'But that doesn't mean it's easy to accept.'

Ivy didn't answer, not because she didn't know what to say, but because she didn't need to. All the years the two of them had wasted over a silly fall out melted away, and it was like it had always been between them. 'I'm so glad you are my friend, Laurie.'

'Ooh, don't,' Laurie said as she flapped a hand in front of her face. 'Or I'll be the one crying.' They both laughed. 'I really am sorry I let that idiot come between us, you know.'

Laurie had fallen hard and fast for a summer visitor back when they were teenagers. She'd refused to listen to anyone, Ivy included, who suspected he was using her as nothing more than an amusement for the duration of the summer. Laurie had been convinced she'd found "the one" and after she'd been left high and dry, Ivy had avoided speaking to her until it was far too late. 'I know,' she said, wrinkling her nose in sympathy at her friend's past plight. 'And I'm sorry I didn't try harder sooner, but Mum had a rough couple of months and by the time she was feeling better, I didn't know what to say that wouldn't sound like I told you so, and that would've been the last thing you needed.'

'Even though it was true.' Laurie shrugged and picked up her glass. 'It's all water under the bridge now. I've got Jake and he's everything I could ever wish for.' She gave Ivy a knowing look. 'Well, most of the time.'

Ivy laughed and raised her glass to chink it against Laurie's. 'To your almost perfect boyfriend.'

After they'd put their drinks down, Laurie reached for the bottle and topped them both up with a couple more inches of wine. 'I'm just keeping it cold,' she said with a cheeky smile when Ivy protested they'd both be drunk if they weren't careful.

'So, is it just you and your mum for Christmas?' Laurie asked once she'd settled the bottle back amongst the ice in the bucket.

Ivy nodded, feeling a little melancholy once more. 'We're

going to try and make it the best possible time we can until she goes into the hospice. I'm going to go through the TV planner tomorrow and download a bunch of films we can watch together.'

'That sounds like a great idea. Mum and I do that now and again and it's so much fun. You should have a look on the Arts channel because we found loads of Christmas concerts and things as well – lots of easy watching.'

Ivy made a mental note to do just that. 'Sounds like a great idea.'

'My folks are doing their usual monster buffet on Boxing Day. I don't suppose your mum will be up to it, but there'll be so many leftovers I could put a box of stuff together and Mum and I could pop over for a couple of hours on the 27th or 28th.'

Laurie hesitated, as though worried she'd pushed things too far, when instead Ivy was staying quiet because she was momentarily overwhelmed by the kindness of the offer. 'It's up to you, if you'd rather just have the two of you then I'll completely understand.'

'Pinch me again,' Ivy said with a watery laugh.

'Sorry, sorry! I forgot about not being nice,' Laurie said, looking a bit teary-eyed herself. 'I just thought...'

'I know. And, thank you, it sounds like a lovely idea.' Ivy took a fortifying sip of her wine and let the ice cold liquid rest in her mouth a moment before she swallowed it down. 'Mum's gung-ho about me selling the house after...' She left her sentence hanging, unable to say the words.

Laurie's eyes widened in surprise. 'She doesn't want you to leave the Point, does she?'

'No. Nothing like that.' Ivy fumbled in her pocket for the flyer and flattened it out on the table between them.

'Mr Cavendish's place?' Laurie cast her a curious look.

Ivy nodded. 'Mum thinks I should sell the cottage and buy the bookshop.'

Laurie glanced from her face, down to the flyer, then back again, a quizzical frown etched between her brows. 'But do you even *want* to run a bookshop? I know we always loved going in there when we were kids, but I didn't think it was something you hankered after.'

Ivy laughed. 'It's not. Mum thinks I should expand the stuff I'm doing now into a proper retail space. It would be nice to have a bit more room than our back bedroom, but it feels like a lot to try and take on.'

Laurie turned her attention back to the flyer. 'It would be a shame to lose the bookshop all together, perhaps you could do a combination of both?' As she warmed to her subject she began to nod along with her thoughts. 'Mr Cavendish hasn't changed the place in all the years we've been going in there so it's screaming out for an overhaul. There's enough floorspace for plenty of bookshelves and still have somewhere to display your clothing and furniture. Maximising the offering would appeal to a broader customer base too, so you'd be able to sell across to people who come in for one thing. A bit like we do with the gift shop and the café.'

'Slow down, slow down,' Ivy protested with a laugh as she raised both hands to ward off the barrage of ideas. 'I don't even know if I want to sell the cottage.' She swallowed hard. 'I don't know if I can bear to even think about it at the moment.'

Laurie patted her leg, her eager expression shifting to one of contrition. 'Sorry, I got a bit carried away with myself there. I can't see Mr Cavendish finding a buyer in a hurry, it's not the right time of year to try and sell a business. Anyone from outside the village would take one look at how quiet it is and likely be put off. Maybe you could have a chat with him after Christmas and ask him to let you know if anyone else shows an interest? At least that way you'd have time to make a counter-offer. I'm sure he'd like to keep the place in the hands of someone local if at all possible.'

None of which had even occurred to Ivy, and she said as much. 'You're right. It's not a decision I need to rush into. Let's forget about all that for now and just enjoy ourselves.' She pushed the flyer to the edge of the table. 'Now, tell me all about how things are going with Jake.'

They'd worked their way through two-thirds of the bottle when Ivy noticed Laurie's attention shift towards a commotion at the door. From the light in her eyes, Ivy didn't need to look round to know it must be Jake, but she turned in her seat anyway to watch the three tall men weaving their way across the crowded pub, their progress hindered by the number of people wanting to pet the golden retriever who was bringing up the rear of their little group. Jake reached their table first, leaning over to plant a kiss on Laurie's lips before claiming the chair opposite her. Ivy raised her hand in a little wave of greeting when he managed to look away from Laurie for two seconds to acknowledge her. 'Hi.'

'Hello.' He released Laurie's hands and offered one to her. 'It's nice to finally meet you.'

'You too. I've been hearing all about you.' Ivy winced then laughed as Laurie aimed a kick at her ankle beneath the table.

'Been spilling all your secrets, sis?' Nick shook his head in Laurie's direction as he edged into the narrow gap between the tables and bussed a kiss on Ivy's cheek. 'Hello, you.'

There was such warmth in his smile that for a moment Ivy felt a pang about what might have been. 'Hello, yourself.'

'Come on, Nick, make yourself useful and get the drinks in,' Alex said as he all but grabbed the other man and tugged him out of the gap. 'Three pints and another bottle of whatever our beautiful companions are having.' He fished into his wallet as he spoke and pulled out a couple of notes.

Nick waved him off. 'Next round is on you, I've got these.' He'd plunged into the crowd at the bar before Ivy could protest that she wasn't sure she needed any more wine.

'Ivy, my love, my heart, how are you?' Alex asked as he wormed his way onto the bench seat beside her and draped a somewhat over-familiar arm round her shoulders. 'When are you going to put me out of my misery and say you'll run away with me?'

God, he was incorrigible, but the wicked gleam in his eyes held nothing but humour and kindness. 'About the same time an actual mermaid walks out of the ocean and onto the beach,' she replied, unhooking his arm and placing it in his lap with a friendly pat.

'So fair and yet so cruel.' Alex clutched at his heart as though he'd suffered a fatal blow, but he was laughing all the while.

There was something different about him and for a moment she couldn't put her finger on it. 'You shaved off your beard!'

Grinning, Alex raised a hand to rub his chin. 'It was driving me mad, if I'm honest with you.' His eyes took on a wicked gleam. 'Besides, the clean-shaven look is much kinder on a lady's gentle skin when I kiss her under the mistletoe.'

Don't blush, don't blush. It was hard not to, though, when he was looking at her like he wanted to eat her up. And she was more than half-way inclined to let him. Hiding the dangerous thought with a quick sip from her glass, Ivy decided she'd best face him down before they did something they'd both regret later. 'Ha! You should be so lucky.'

'In my dreams, Ivy, in my dreams.' Alex gave her leg a quick pat as if to reassure her he was only teasing then something on the table caught his eye. 'Hey, what's this?'

Ivy could only watch with a faint sense of dread as he slid the details for Mr Cavendish's bookshop closer and began to read. Though his flirting was harmless and sweetly meant, Ivy didn't know him well enough to feel comfortable talking about where the flyer had come from. 'Oh, I don't know, it was on the table when we sat down.'

Leaning forward, she made a show of reading it over his shoulder, feeling the lie settle uncomfortably in the pit of her stomach. A quick glance to the left confirmed Laurie was too caught up in whatever she and Jake were talking about to pay attention, and she swallowed down the little bubble of guilt. It was more a fib, than a lie, nothing to worry about. 'It's for one of the local shops. I guess Mr Cavendish is ready to retire.'

She hoped he'd leave it at that, but Alex picked up the sheet of paper and began to study it more closely. 'I don't remember seeing a bookshop on the seafront.' He sounded distracted, as though he was thinking out loud rather than speaking directly to her.

'It's tucked away in one of the side streets, so it's not surprising you haven't come across it.' There was something about the way he continued to study the flyer that unnerved her, and she had to fight the impulse to snatch it out of his hand. 'You're not in the market for a bookshop, are you?'

She waited for him to laugh, to deny the idea as preposterous and set the flyer back on the table. Instead, he folded it carefully and tucked it away in the inside pocket of his jacket. 'Stranger things have happened,' he said, again sounding more as if he was talking to himself.

The discomfort in her middle took on a slightly sick edge now and Ivy made a grab for her wine. *Tell him. Tell him now that you're thinking about buying it.* Ignoring the urging of her inner voice, Ivy took a sip from her glass and tried to pretend everything was fine.

Tried to pretend that the man whose hip was pressed against hers hadn't just tucked all her hopes and dreams for the future away in his pocket with the look of a man who'd just stumbled across a dream of his own.

Merry bloody Christmas, Ivy.

7

ANDREW

'More champagne, Tom?' Andrew Morgan raised the bottle in his hand as he asked the question, almost spilling it when his elbow bumped into someone behind him. Glancing over his shoulder he saw his son wedged into the corner next to Alex. Nick was playfully clutching his ribs and pulling a face.

'Steady on, Dad,' Nick said with a rueful grin.

'Well, you shouldn't be hanging round the place like a bad smell. There's another bottle in the fridge, make yourself useful and see if Archie and Philippa need a top up.' Tom's father and step-mother were an essential part of their ever-expanding family circle, and Andrew wanted them well taken care of.

'I've only just fought my way to the buffet.' Nick raised a plate laden with cold meat, sausage rolls, thick home-cut chips hot from the deep fat fryer, and pickles in protest. 'Besides, everyone knows where the fridge is.'

Andrew raised a brow and stared at his son. He didn't need to say anything. Nick understood the rules when it came to hosting guests under Andrew's roof. With a put-upon sigh, Nick hid his plate on a shelf in the wall unit and sloped off towards the kitchen. Hid might be an optimistic word because no sooner was his son's back turned than Alex filched two sausage rolls from the plate and stuffed them into his mouth. With a laugh and a shake of his head, Andrew turned back to Tom. 'Where were we?'

Tom covered the top of his glass with a hand. 'I'm on call so I won't, thanks. Nice jumper by the way.'

'Thank you.' Andrew stroked a proud hand over the front of his garish Christmas jumper. It might be hotter than Hades with the heating on and a house full of guests, but he wasn't going to let that get in the way of a family tradition. He had a wardrobe full of them, and this year's cross-eyed reindeer with fairy lights festooning its antlers had been a gift from Laurie and Jake. 'You'll have to ask Nerissa to get you one next year.'

'I think that's a great idea,' his sister deadpanned, and Andrew had to swallow his own smile. They'd always shared a similar sense of humour and Tom's slightly horrified look as he glanced between the two of them only enhanced his enjoyment of the moment.

'Well, I wouldn't want to steal your thunder or anything,' Tom said in the strained tones of a man grasping at straws.

'Nonsense. You're one of the family now! In fact, you're welcome to nip upstairs and borrow one from my collection.'

Tom gave a frantic shake of his head. 'I'm on call, remember.'

'Oh, I don't know,' Nerissa mused as she eyed him up and down. 'The patients might appreciate a festive touch.' And then she blew it by bursting out laughing. 'Oh, lord, the look on your face!'

Tom narrowed his eyes at them before a broad grin stretched his mouth. 'You had me there for a minute.'

Laughing, Andrew held up his free hand to his sister so they could share a high five. 'That deserves a refill.'

'Definitely,' Nerissa agreed, thrusting her glass out. 'We can't let good champagne go to waste.'

Though Tom lowered his voice as he leaned towards Nerissa, Andrew still heard him ask, 'Does that mean I'll have to carry you to bed later?' Nerissa's cheeks pinkened and the smitten look she gave Tom might have made Andrew roll his eyes if he wasn't so bloody delighted for the pair of them. His darling little sister had been on her own for too damn long and he'd forgive Tom almost anything just to see the light shining in her eyes.

'Let me take that empty glass for you then,' Andrew offered before he embarrassed them all by tugging the couple into a bear hug. 'I've got some alcohol-free beer in the fridge. Or there's sparkling water, or a can of Coke, if you'd prefer?'

'I'll take a Coke, thanks.' Tom handed him the glass then glanced round the packed room. 'I didn't think you'd fit us all in, but you've managed it somehow.' As well as Tom's extended family, they'd invited Tony, Andrew's brother-in-law who'd bought his long-term partner, Debra with him, and Jake's mother, Linda. There was barely room to breathe, never mind sit but everyone had found themselves a bit of space. A small frown creased Tom's brow. 'Where are the kids?'

Andrew gave him a reassuring smile, having passed them on his way into the room. 'They're camped out halfway up the stairs with their iPads and a plate Sylvia put together for them. Toby's keeping watch.'

'On their food, no doubt,' Nerissa said with an exasperated roll of her eyes.

'Sylvia thought of that, and he's got his own bowl of treats so the kids can eat in peace.'

Tom was still frowning. 'They ought to make a bit of an effort to be sociable.'

Andrew shook his head. 'When my two were that age you

couldn't pry them out of their rooms to hang out with a load of boring oldies like us. Relax and stop fretting. We're all family here, and Sylvia and I will keep an eye on them. I'll get you that Coke and you concentrate on making sure my sister is having a good time.'

With a grin, Tom slid an arm round Nerissa's waist. 'Well, if you insist.'

Andrew didn't get very far on his mission to fetch Tom's drink. He edged out of the living room to find Nick in the hallway with the fresh bottle of champagne in one hand and what looked like a business card in the other. Eyes wide in shock, he kept staring from the card to Laurie and Jake who were standing next to him, matching grins on their faces. 'What's all this?' Andrew asked, though he already knew because Laurie had talked to him and Sylvia about it. Laurie had wanted to double-check they really wouldn't take the money from the savings account she and Nick had set up. As if they'd take a penny from them! It was enough to know they'd cared sufficiently to set some of their hard-earned cash aside with the intention of repaying some of the household expenses. The shop did fine – more than fine after a very successful summer and he and his wife had agreed the kids needed every penny for themselves. Besides, they'd been mortgage-free since his mum had passed, thanks to his share of the proceeds they'd made after selling her cottage. He and Nerissa had contemplated keeping it as a holiday let, but had decided they had too much on their plates as it was.

'Laurie and Jake want to invest in the warehouse conversion!' Nick showed him the business card. It was white with a simple silhouette of a mermaid in the top corner and the words:

MERMAID DEVELOPMENTS

Nick Morgan – Managing Director

'It's just something I mocked-up on the computer,' Jake said, with a sheepish grin. 'We wanted to surprise Nick with something when we told him.' He turned to Nick. 'I'll help you with a proper design once you've decided what to call your new enterprise.'

'Nothing wrong with Mermaid Designs. It fits in with the theme of the rest of the family businesses.' Nick turned back to Andrew, words tumbling over each other. 'With Laurie and Jake's money as collateral, I'll be in a much stronger position when I'm talking to the bank. I really think I can pull it off.' He turned back to his sister and Jake with a bewildered smile. 'Are you sure you're sure about this?'

Jake laughed. 'We're sure. I spoke to Mum as well, because some of that is money she's given me, and she's thrilled about it. We don't need it just now, do we?' He glanced down at Laurie who shook her head as she leaned into him.

'No. We're not in a rush to do anything right now. We love the cottage, and the Walkers have agreed we can stay as long as we want. Work is our focus for the next couple of years. The Christmas food I did proved such a success I want to look into doing more catering and Jake's thinking about writing a book alongside his work for the paper, so we've got more than enough to keep us going.'

'Don't bother.' At Alex's sardonic comment they all turned to face him where'd he paused at the foot of the stairs. 'The book, I mean,' he continued. 'Listen to the voice of experience, and save yourself a world of pain.'

Andrew watched him make his way up the stairs, and when Alex paused to say something to his niece and nephew, he leaned closer to the others and murmured, 'I didn't know Alex had written a book, did you?'

Nick and Jake exchanged matching looks of surprise. The pair of them had grown close with Alex in the past couple of months, being of similar age and sharing the same laidback sense of humour. 'First I've heard of it,' Nick said.

'I wonder why.' Jake rubbed his chin, his gaze fixed on Alex's back. 'I'll have to do some digging.' Given his background as an investigative journalist, if anyone could get to the bottom of things, it would be Jake.

'Right, I've left poor Tom waiting for a drink long enough, and you need to see to Archie, Phillipa, and the rest of our guests,' Andrew said to Nick, nodding at the full bottle in his hand. 'Wonderful news about the conversion, Son, I know you'll make a great success of it.'

Nick leaned in to brush a quick kiss on Andrew's cheek. 'Thanks, Dad. Would you mind coming with me when I chat to Liam about the plans? You might think of something I'll miss.'

Andrew's heart swelled with love and admiration for this beloved boy of his. Though he had a working relationship with the architect from when they'd converted the shop to make space for Laurie's café, Andrew suspected Nick was more than capable of handling himself and was just looking for an excuse to make him feel included. 'Whatever I can do to help, you only have to ask. Message me the date once you've fixed it up and I'll be there with bells on.'

'I won't be much use with the technical side of things, but I can hump and dump stuff if you need an extra pair of hands,' Jake offered, and Andrew's heart gave another huge thump at the generosity of this man who was becoming as much of a son to him as if he were his own flesh and blood.

'Here's a thought,' Andrew mused. 'Laurie and your mum are off to visit Jen and Ivy tomorrow. Why don't the three of us take a wander down to the warehouse and you can talk Jake and me through your latest ideas for the place.'

Nick beamed. 'Sounds like a plan. Cheers, Dad.'

Eager to share the latest update with his wife, Andrew followed the sound of 'Rocking Around the Christmas Tree' into the kitchen. The memory of him and Sylvia dancing to it with the kids filled his head. Nick couldn't have been more than five, and Laurie had still been small enough that Andrew had held her in his arms as they'd jigged about to the silly song. The kitchen had always been the heart of their home, and all his favourite family memories were of the four of them sitting round the battered wooden table. He had to pause and catch his breath at the bitter-sweet realisation that once Nick had converted the warehouse into flats, he'd be moving out. It was past time for him to be setting up his own home, Andrew knew, but how many more Christmases would there be with all his family under one roof? He glanced over to where Sylvia stood at the sink, already washing up a few plates and glasses she must've collected while he was chatting. He knew he should be grateful for more time to spend just the two of them, but he hated the thought of their nest being finally empty. He'd not said anything to her, because he wasn't sure how to without potentially hurting her feelings. Well, there'd be time enough to sort it out, it wasn't like Nick would be leaving for months yet. No point borrowing sorrows when there was a party to be enjoyed.

Speaking of which... 'Leave those bits, my love, and come and have a drink with me. You haven't stopped all morning.' Andrew headed for the fridge to grab Tom his Coke but froze in his tracks when Sylvia gave a telltale sniffle. Hurrying over, Andrew curled his arms round her from behind. He tried to catch her gaze over her shoulder, but she wouldn't look up at him. 'Hey, hey, now. What's the matter?'

Sylvia sniffled again before turning in his arms and burying her face in his chest. Her wet, rubber-gloved hands gripped the back of his shirt, soaking the material but he ignored the damp sensation. All he cared about was finding out who or what had dared to upset his wife on what should be a day of celebration. He hugged her tight for a long moment before leaning back to look down at her. 'Come on, darling, tell me what's got you like this?'

Sylvia pressed her face into his chest. 'Pay me no mind, I'm being silly.' He could hear laughter through the tears and some of his tension inside eased.

'Tell me, anyway,' he coaxed. Stroking a hand over her hair, he rubbed the back of her neck before shifting his hold so he could cup her chin and lift her tear-stained face. She didn't wear a lot of makeup, but her eyeliner had spread a bit, so he wiped beneath each eye with a tender thumb. 'Beautiful.' He pressed a kiss to the tip of her nose. 'As beautiful as the day I met you.'

She snorted a laugh through her reddened nose. 'You pulled my pigtails.'

'Got your attention, though.' And he'd done his best to keep it ever since. 'Now, what's got into you?'

After tugging off her rubber gloves and tossing them next to the sink, Sylvia pulled a tissue from her pocket, dabbed her nose and sighed. 'I overheard Laurie telling Nick about the money, and he sounded so excited.'

'It's been a while since we've heard him happy, eh?' Though they hadn't been able to get him to open up about it, they knew Nick had suffered a real blow to the heart over the summer. Aurora Storm had recruited him to help stage her mermaid video stunts and they'd had a bit of a fling. They suspected it had been more than a bit of a fling for Nick, truth be told, and he'd been restless ever since. For a while they'd worried he would chuck it all in and chase after Aurora all the way to London. But when he didn't hear any more from the pop star after she'd left town, Nick had become increasingly withdrawn. Andrew thought he was well shot of her, outraged at the way she'd used and abused Nick's trust. She'd gone so far as to leak the news about the stunts to the press, letting the family believe Jake had betrayed them in the process. As far as Andrew was concerned it was great that with Laurie and Jake's support, Nick could hopefully throw himself into the conversion project and have something positive to focus on.

'I've been so worried about him,' Sylvia said, echoing his thoughts. 'It was nice to hear him laugh again.'

She didn't look as happy about it as she might have done, and Andrew knew there was more to it than that. 'Tell me the rest.'

Sylvia laughed. 'I don't know why I ever try and keep anything hidden from you, Andrew Morgan, because you can read me like a book.'

'It's my job to look out for you, my love.' Reaching out, he drew her against his chest and pressed a kiss to the top of her head. 'Always has been, always will be.'

She wrapped her arms round his waist and sighed again. 'I just got to thinking about what it'd be like this time next year and how we'll be rattling around the place by ourselves.'

It was Andrew's turn to chuckle. 'I've been thinking the same thing, only I wasn't quite sure how to bring it up.' He hugged his wife tight. 'We've raised two wonderful children; we should be happy to see them making their way in the world.'

'Oh, I am, and it'll be lovely to have the place to ourselves.' She was sounding despondent again.

Pulling back so he could catch her eyes, Andrew waggled his eyebrows. 'Just think of all the games of strip poker we'll be able to play,' he said, earning a slap on the arm along with the laughter he'd known it would bring. 'Seriously, though, we'll have plenty to keep us busy. We've got our weekends with Emily and Max to look forward to.' They'd been more than happy to suggest it to Tom after the success of the previous weekend. It would allow Nerissa and Tom some alone time as well as give himself and Sylvia a chance to spoil them a bit.

Sylvia's smile widened. 'Yes. It'll be lovely to have them here on a regular basis. And there's one or two other families in the village who might benefit from the odd respite break.' Her expression clouded. 'I'm not sure what the school would feel about that, though.' Sylvia had been helping out as a teaching assistant at the village primary since their own two had been young enough to go there.

He touched her cheek, thinking he'd never loved her more than he did in this moment. She had so much love for everyone. 'Perhaps we should have a chat with some of your contacts in child services and look into something more formal like fostering – if you want to?' There were so many children in need of support, it broke his heart to think about it.

'I'd love that.' Sylvia was all smiles once more as she reached up and linked her arms at the back of his neck. 'And who knows, in a few years' time, we might have a grandbaby or two to look after.'

Andrew lowered his forehead to rest against hers. 'Whatever life has in store for us, my love, I know it'll be a blessing because I get to spend it with you.' He pressed a tender kiss against each of her tear-bruised eyelids, on her nose and then a deeper one to her mouth.

'How did I ever get so lucky?' she sighed when they came up for air.

The endless parade of Christmas tunes on the radio was interrupted by the smooth tones of the resident DJ:

And here it is folks the new Christmas number one, and who else would it be other than our very own Aurora Storm, with

'Home again'.

Whatever resentment he might harbour for the woman, there was no denying she could sing. Holding Sylvia tight against him, Andrew began to shuffle in slow circles in time to the lilting melody. 'I wished for you, you know?' he murmured against Sylvia's brow.

She tilted her head back to look at him. 'What do you mean?'

'All those years ago when I knew you were the one for me, I went down to the caves, threw a coin into the sea and asked the mermaids to help me win your heart.'

Sylvia's eyes grew round. 'You never told me that! How is this the first time in thirty years you've thought to tell me?'

He shrugged. 'I haven't thought about it in years, not until young Max got himself in trouble trying to ask the mermaids for help after damaging his mother's blanket.' The poor kid had been cut off by the tide and only a concerted rescue effort by the family, and members of the community who'd come running the moment they heard, had got him safely back on dry land. 'And then I was thinking just now of Aurora and that daft stunt she pulled posing as a mermaid, and I remembered again.'

'And are you still glad you made that wish?' Sylvia's tone was teasing, because if there was one thing she never needed to doubt it was how much her husband loved her.

Andrew made a show of considering it, earning himself a pinch on the backside. 'Ouch! I reckon I got my money's worth.' Laughing, he pressed a kiss to her lips. 'If I'd known it was going to be this good, I'd have gone the whole hog and chucked them a pound coin instead of 50p.' He captured her outraged protest in another kiss and decided perhaps they didn't need to rush into bringing anyone else into the house once Nick moved out.

Nick did a quick circuit of the lounge with the champagne before depositing the half-full bottle on a table next to the sofa where Archie and Philippa were sharing a plate of sausage rolls, mini-Yorkshire puddings stuffed with roast beef and horseradish, and smoked salmon slices on neat squares of brown bread. Linda was perched on the arm of the sofa, chatting with Uncle Tony and Debra about a cruise she was planning in the new year. 'I can trust you to look after this, can't I?' Nick said, giving Philippa a wink. He might not be in the Christmas spirit, but the news Laurie and Jake had just sprung upon him had cheered him up no end.

'Oh, it'll be in very safe hands, darling, don't you worry,' she replied with an answering grin. She looked at his now empty hands and frowned. 'But what about you? You must make sure you enjoy yourself, too.'

'Grab yourself a glass and come and join us.' Archie patted the spare seat beside him. 'Tom was telling us about the boat trips you run. I wouldn't mind a fishing trip sometime.'

Nick declined the seat with a polite smile. 'I need to find out what's happened to Dad with Tom's drink and then I've promised Nerissa I'll take Toby out for a quick walk, but I'll join you in a bit. And as far as the fishing goes, once the weather's better, I'll be more than happy to take you out. Mate's rates, of course.'

'Mate's rates?' Archie snorted. 'That's no way to run a business, boy. I'll pay the going rate for a private day charter and that's the end of the matter.'

Nick gave him a relieved thumbs up. 'Cheers, Archie. You're a gentleman.' It was always a bit awkward talking about money with friends and family. But it was something he was going to have to get used to if Laurie and Jake really were going to back him over the warehouse development. He could talk more about it with Jake tomorrow, see how he wanted to handle things in terms of contracts, or whatever. 'Right, do you need anything else while I'm in the kitchen?'

'We're fine, thank you, darling.' Philippa raised her glass towards him. 'Happy Boxing Day.'

He laughed and raised an imaginary glass in return. 'And to you, both. I'll see you when I'm back from my walk.'

Catching Tom's eye as he made his way from the room, he grinned when the other man raised his hands to his throat and made a gasping motion. 'I'm on it!' As he passed the dining room, he remembered his abandoned plate of food and decided it wouldn't do any harm to do a quick mine sweep of the buffet table on his way. He took one step inside, his hungry gaze locked on the tray of mini-Yorkshires, then realised he wasn't alone. Tucked into the corner and shielded from view behind the open door, Laurie and Jake were locked in the kind of embrace no man ever needed to see his sister in. With a quick mournful glance at the buffet table, Nick beat a retreat before either of them had chance to notice him.

Though he'd had his doubts about Jake at first, it was as plain as the nose on his face that he and Laurie had made a real love match. He also liked the way Jake respected his sister, both personally and professionally. The café was Laurie's business and other than being happy to stick on an apron and help out when it got really busy, Jake had shown no signs of interfering or trying to make 'helpful' suggestions about how she might do things better. He was also starting to make a mark for himself at the local paper and had asked Nick's opinion the other night over drinks for suggestions of investigative pieces which could highlight things that really mattered to the community. To Nick it seemed like Jake was serious about making a go of it in the Point. Though they'd told him earlier they weren't in a rush to make any changes, Nick privately expected there'd be talk of an engagement before too much longer.

He would be delighted for them if – when – that came to pass because he adored Laurie and wanted nothing more than to see her happy and settled. Still, her happiness was a painful contrast to his own situation. She was six years younger than him yet so much more in control of her life. Nick raised a hand to cover the breast pocket of his checked shirt where he'd tucked away the business card they'd made for him. His love life might be as barren as the rocks beneath the Point, but at least he had plans. Much as he loved his folks, it was well past time he had a home of his own – even if he had to resort to building one for himself. As for finding someone to share that home with him... No, he would not think about her. Not today.

The universe had other ideas, it seemed, because as he entered the kitchen he instantly recognised the husky voice coming from the radio. How could he not when it haunted his dreams, and too many of his waking moments, if he was going to be honest with himself? To add insult to injury, his folks were slow dancing to Aurora's latest hit, like a pair of teenagers at a school disco. Did his mother really have her hands tucked in the back pockets of his dad's jeans? *Pass the brain bleach*!

'Pretend I'm not here!' he said in a loud voice as he raised a hand to shield his eyes and hurried towards the fridge to finally get Tom his Coke.

'Don't worry, we will,' his dad replied cheerfully, arms still wrapped round his mum. 'Don't let the door hit you on the way out.'

Nick closed the door behind him, but not before the chorus of 'Home Again' reached him:

'No matter how far, no matter how long we are apart, I'll hold tight to the dream of you, until I'm home again'.

Closing his eyes, Nick pressed his back to the wall until he could breathe past the fist of longing clenched round his heart. Three weeks. How could it be possible to fall hopelessly in love with someone in such a short space of time?

When Aurora had dismissed him with a quick peck on the cheek and the words, 'it's been fun, Nico,' before hopping in the back of her Range Rover with the blacked-out windows and disappearing - quite literally – into the sunset, he'd sworn to forget about her.

As the summer's heat faded, he'd told himself it was a stupid infatuation, that *who* she was had affected his thinking and he'd blown their love affair out of proportion.

Once the bitter autumn storms started smashing against the group of islands known locally as the Seven Sisters where he'd helped Aurora stage her first mermaid hoax, he'd come to the grim realisation that his feelings for her were as stubborn as those rocks. He had no choice other than to weather the storm of his disappointment until brighter days came once more.

As he pulled himself together and forced a smile he didn't feel, Nick observed ruefully that things might be easier if everyone round him wasn't so sickeningly loved-up. Even Aunt Nerissa, who he'd relied upon to support him in the forever-single corner had fallen head over heels after more than twenty years on her own.

And she'd never looked better, he thought as he approached her and Tom and handed the doctor his long-awaited drink. 'Sorry, for the terrible service,' he said as Tom swiped the can and made a show of gulping a mouthful. 'I blame the staff.'

Nerissa reached out and untucked the collar tip of Nick's shirt which had got twisted somehow and smoothed it out in a gesture which turned into a gentle caress. 'Are you all right, Nicky? You look a bit tired.'

She'd always seen into the heart of him, ever since he was a little boy. And unlike most people, she couldn't be deflected by a cheeky smile and an outrageous comment, so Nick settled for honesty. 'I'm getting there, one step at a time and all that.'

Her hand rested on his shoulder for a minute before she accepted what he'd said with a nod. 'That's all any of us can do.' Her smile brightened. 'Are you sure you don't mind taking Toby out for a bit? He's being very well behaved but I'm not sure how much longer we can keep him distracted. Left to his own devices he'll be hoovering up sausage rolls any minute.'

'He's not the only one,' Nick said with a grin as he snatched one from the plate Tom was holding. 'In fact, if *Laurie and Jake*,' he raised his voice as he turned his head towards the open dining room door, 'are quite finished, I'll wrap up a few to sustain me on my walk.'

A few seconds later, his sister emerged from the dining room, trying to capture her suspiciously tangled hair up in a ponytail. Jake followed on her heels, rubbing the back of his hand across his lips to remove traces of Laurie's pink lipstick. 'Did you want me for something?' she asked Nick, studiously ignoring the wicked grin he couldn't resist plastering on his face.

'Only for you to vacate the dining room so the poor, starving masses can eat something!' Accepting the mock-shove Jake gave him with a laugh, Nick slipped past them. Surveying the buffet with a greedy eye, he grabbed a couple of napkins from a pile and proceeded to fill each with tasty treats from the tempting selection. Spirits lifted by the prospect of finally getting something to eat, Nick wove his way back through the crowded lounge and out into the hall. He put the food down on the table near the door only long enough to shrug on his padded, water-proof jacket, then tucked the bulging napkins in the front pockets of the coat. The rattle of the dog's lead as he unhooked it stirred Toby from his spot at the bottom of the stairs. Abandoning his watch on the kids' plates, he began circling Nick, trying to catch the end of his lead between his teeth.

'Want some company?' It was Alex who was squatting behind his nephew on the stairs, watching whatever the boy was engrossed in on his iPad.

Nick really didn't, but it would be rude to refuse. 'Up to you, mate.'

Whether it was something in his tone, or whether Alex had only offered to be polite, the other man shrugged and said: 'I'll stick with *Avengers Endgame* then, if that's all right with you?'

'Don't blame you,' Nick replied with a grateful smile. 'I won't be long, anyway. Straight down the hill and back again. Mum's got a rhubarb crumble in the oven and I'm not giving you lot a chance to wolf it all down before I can get my share. Don't think I didn't notice how many of the filo prawns you ate.'

Alex rubbed his belly. 'You snooze, you lose.'

'Shh.' Max tugged at his uncle's sleeve. 'You're missing a really good bit.'

'Sorry,' Alex whispered before he glanced back over at Nick and touched a finger to his watch, made a walking gesture with his two fingers then raised his hand to mime having a drink. Giving him a quick thumbs up, Nick clipped on Toby's lead and let the excited retriever out the front door.

It didn't take long to reach the seafront, the five-minute stroll it usually took shortened by the eager pull of the dog against his lead. 'All right, all right,' Nick said with a laugh as they jogged down the steps to the beach. 'Here we are.' A quick glance left and right told him they pretty much had the place to themselves so he was happy to let the dog run free. Toby was well behaved, and Nick had never had trouble calling him back, as long as he kept in ear shot it would be fine. Toby shot off like a rocket, his happy barks echoing round the empty beach as he made a dash straight for the soft sand which separated the pebbles from the sea.

Nick followed at a more leisurely pace, happy to enjoy the emptiness round him after the packed, noisy chaos of home. He loved a good party as well as the next man, but there was only so much of other people's happiness he could take these days. *And whose fault was that?* Dipping a hand in his pocket, Nick fished out a sausage roll and stuffed it glumly into his mouth. It was no good blaming Aurora. She'd never made him any promises, after all. His gaze roamed across the open water and out to the little cluster of islands beyond, almost hidden by a thick bank of cloud. He remembered the day he'd first taken Aurora out on his boat as if it had been yesterday. He'd watched in awe as she'd transformed herself from a pretty girl no different to any other he might pass on the street to sultry, seductive siren with one expert application of stage makeup and a long, glossy wig. The change had been electric, and a little unsettling until he'd had to help her wrestle into the six-foot long mermaid's tail that completed her outfit – the pair of them almost slipping off the rocks at the base of the one of the islands in the process.

Her laughter, that was what he remembered most from that day. A pure peel of joy when they'd been messing round during the filming, and then something deeper, richer and full of sleepy satisfaction when she'd curled up against his chest that night, after she'd invited him to join her in the room she'd booked in a budget travel hotel just off the motorway. He'd been surprised – expecting she'd have squirreled herself away in a private rental somewhere, but she'd told him it was easier to hide in plain sight. After all, she'd been out of the public eye for a couple of years at that point – long enough to fade in most people's memories - and who would expect to find even a has-been pop star in their local Travelodge? And so it had proven even when they'd ventured beyond her bed to explore the local area and dine out here and there. He'd avoided taking her anywhere in the Point itself, preferring to guard his privacy as much as her own. Luckily people had been too distracted by the budding romance between his sister and Jake to pay much attention to what he'd been doing.

Sinking down on the stones above the waterline, Nick hooked his arms round his knees and sighed. What was he going to do? Pretending not to think about Aurora was getting him nowhere. He reached into his pocket and pulled out his phone. He stared at the blank screen for a long time before unlocking it and flicking open WhatsApp. The last message from Aurora was dated back in July.

It's sorted.

She'd sent it after he'd called to warn her Jake had uncovered her identity and was writing a story about it. When she'd been splashed all over the headlines the next day, Nick had been furious, and wanted to knocked Jake flat on his arse when he came crawling the next morning trying to apologise to Laurie for betraying them all. Only it had turned out later that Aurora had been the source of the story – issuing a slick press statement to all the tabloids to ensure maximum exposure before dropping her new single. Back with a bang, she'd raced to the top of the charts and been there ever since. And he'd never heard a word in all that time.

Nick thumbed off his phone. She'd probably changed her number by now, so what was the point even thinking about it. His fingers tightened round the handset. Wouldn't it be better to know for sure? Perhaps if she told him to get lost he'd finally be able to shake off this stupid crush once and for all. A snowflake hit the screen, sticking for an instant before melting into a water droplet. Another landed, followed by a third. Tilting his head back, Nick stared in wonder at the fluffy patches of white drifting from the grey clouds above. It almost never snowed in the Point. He could count on the fingers of one hand the number of times it had, and never at Christmas. Toby barked, drawing Nick's attention and he couldn't help but smile at the sight of the dog leaping up to snap at the snow which was beginning to fall more steadily. Raising his phone he took a few photos, wanting to capture the moment of innocent joy.

On a whim, he reactivated the app, uploaded one of the photos and typed a quick message before he could talk himself out of it again:

Merry Christmas, Aurora x Congratulations on your #1. Nick xxxx

9

AURORA

As the audiobook she'd been listening to rolled through the end credits, Aurora sat up and stretched her stiff back. She'd been so caught up in the dramatic final chapters of the story that she hadn't noticed the awkward ball she'd scrunched herself into in the window seat of the pretty apartment she'd rented overlooking the Thames. A chill struck through the glass beside her, but she liked the spot too much to move so she bent her legs up under her chin and tugged her thick Arran sweater down over her knees, then wrapped her arms round them. Pressing her forehead to the glass she could see people moving below. Bright spots of colour against the leaden grey pavement, they hurried along in little groups or moved at a slower pace in strolling pairs – lovers enjoying the crisp, winter air left by an overnight flurry of snow. An enterprising child had gathered enough snow on the roof garden of one of the buildings opposite to build a miniature snowman on their outside table.

Bare trees lining the street had been festooned with white,

fairy lights, their glittering glow adding to the festive atmosphere even though it would be another few hours before darkness fell. As she watched, one of the couples stopped and turned into each other, his black-clad arms forming a dark band against the sunny yellow of her long winter coat. For a moment Aurora let herself imagine it was her down there, wrapped up against the winter chill enjoying a post-lunch walk with a man who had eyes only for her.

'Always wanting more instead of being grateful for what you do have.'

It was an admonishment from long ago, a ghostly echo of a mother who'd never understood why her child couldn't be satisfied with her lot. *'Nothing wrong with a hard day's graft. If everyone had been born a prince, who'd plough the fields?'*

Aurora couldn't help but laugh at the memory of that one – her mother had never set foot on a farm in her life, preferring the familiar backstreets of the northern town she'd been born and raised in, like generations of their family before her. By the time Aurora had come along, the town's industrial hay days were long past, and jobs were few and far between. Still, her parents hadn't understood the wanderlust deep in Aurora's soul and though they were appreciative of the money she'd been able to give them, they'd refused point blank her offer to buy them a new home somewhere better. *'How could it be better to move to a place where we don't know a living soul?'* her dad had protested with a disbelieving shake of his head. And so she'd left it, knowing at least they'd not have to struggle to make ends meet any more, unlike many of their friends and neighbours.

Turning her attention from the view outside to the large, open floorplan of the apartment Aurora couldn't help but compare its showroom chic to the mismatched, cramped living room where her parents were no doubt sat watching the Boxing Day football. Her dad had splashed out on a satellite dish and full package when she'd sent them a share of her first royalty payment, and if she'd never sent another penny, he'd have been content with that. The money she would've spent on a new home for them had gone instead to the local community – a donation to the working men's club to upgrade their entertainment system so families had a proper set up in the back room many used for wedding receptions, birthdays and celebrations to mark other life events. Another chunk had gone to the town's struggling library, a third to the local school to help with breakfast and after school clubs. All anonymous, at her request. They felt like a drop in the ocean, and never assuaged the lingering guilt that a quirk of fate – a singing voice which had made her stand out since her very first school carol concert – was all that stood between the luxury she enjoyed and the edge of poverty she'd grown up on. Her eyes lingered for a moment on the perfect symmetry of the tree she'd paid a decorator to install. For a moment she longed for the ratty old tree her dad had dragged down from the loft every year that they'd decorated with mismatched baubles and straggly tinsel and wondered if her parents still had it. She dismissed the thought with a sigh. It wouldn't fit in here any more than she'd fit in at home.

Rising from the window seat, Aurora padded barefoot across a navy carpet so thick she left little indentations in her wake and curled up on the white sofa opposite the fireplace. The butter-soft leather welcomed her like a hug, and she nestled back against it with a sigh as she closed her eyes and counted her blessings. Financial security. A job she loved. She thought about her impending tour – the chance to explore the world, fly first class, stay in five-star hotels and eat out at the finest restaurants. Opening her eyes, she turned to look over her shoulder at the solid front door with its sophisticated alarm system beside it. Safety. She was safe now.

Her phone beeped, the two-tone message notification sending her pulse racing so fast Aurora had to raise a hand to her heart to steady herself. *Breathe.* It took a few moments before she could think past the rush of fear and listen to the silent instructions her mind was feeding her. *In for four. Hold for four. Breathe out for four.*

In. Hold. Out.

In. Hold. Out.

Feeling in control once more, Aurora allowed herself a shaky laugh at her foolishness and reached for the phone resting on the smoked-glass coffee table. An unread message indicator showed on her WhatsApp icon. Thinking it was likely Dennis, her agent, with some last-minute itinerary change she flicked it open, only to find the sender was someone she'd never expected to hear from again. Picturing a pair of smiling brown eyes beneath a shock of messy curls, Aurora opened Nick's message, a laugh of delight escaping as she saw the photo of a shaggy golden retriever frolicking in the snow. Still smiling at the happy image she scanned the words below it:

Merry Christmas, Aurora x Congratulations on your #1. Nick xxxx

She stared at the message, not sure what to think other than, why now? Why, after all these months when she'd not heard so much as a peep from him? After she'd had to bring forward the press reveal over her mermaid videos, she'd been caught up in a whirlwind of promotion. From radio and TV interviews to public appearances and – once it was clear she had a huge hit on her hands – some hastily arranged concerts, there'd been barely time to think for the first couple of months. When she had found a moment to herself, her thoughts had strayed too often to the gorgeous, laidback man who'd helped set her back on the path to success – and taught her how to laugh again in the process.

She read the message again. Then a third time. Then a fourth as she tried to decipher its meaning. It was likely nothing more than a friendly greeting, a quick well-wish for the festive season and an acknowledgment of her success. But why then had he added four kisses after his name? Did that mean he was thinking about her and remembering the good times they'd shared? Perhaps even missing her the way she still missed him when she crawled into her empty bed late at night and wished for nothing more than his arms to close round her and ease away the stresses of the day.

Oh, Nick.

Her fingers hovered over the keypad as she wondered what she should say in response when the phone suddenly started ringing. Almost dropping it in shock, Aurora fumbled the handset for a second before spotting her agent's name on the notification bar across the top of the screen. Clicking on answer, she switched it to speakerphone mode. 'Hello, Dennis, how are you?'

'That was quick,' he said, voice sharp with concern. 'Everything all right?' He'd been with her since the very start, seen her through good times and bad... and the very worst.

'Yes, yes, everything's fine. I'd just picked up my phone when you rang so you startled me is all.'

He laughed then, sounding much more relaxed. 'I just wanted to check you were all set for the morning. It's the usual car service, and they'll message you details of the driver and the vehicle when he's on the way.'

Aurora glanced over to the set of matching Louis Vuitton luggage piled up next to the front door. A clear plastic folder rested on the top with her tickets, passport and other essentials neatly filed away. 'All packed and ready to go.' She wished she felt more excited about it. It had been hard work getting back on her feet again, had taken more courage than she'd known she had to step back into the spotlight, but she'd been determined to do it. It was probably just a case of last-minute nerves. Once she got going and was busy with rehearsals and staging for the tour, the adrenaline would start pumping again.

'Great. I should be there in time to meet you, but don't wait if I'm not. Get yourself checked in and into the VIP lounge and I'll find you there if necessary.'

She might have laughed at his mother hen routine, had his attention to detail not once been the very thing that had saved her life. 'I know the drill.' She had to pause for a moment until she could push down the ugly memories that speaking to Dennis always seemed to stir up. It might have been easier if she'd cut ties with him after everything that had happened, but she didn't have many people in her life she could truly trust. 'Thank you, Dennis.'

He was silent for a long time, too, and she knew the same demons that haunted her were plaguing him. 'You never need to thank me,' he said at last, his voice gruff. 'Right, enough of that sentimental bollocks. Early night, my girl, and no booze. You'll be dehydrated enough after the flight to New York, so no need to add a hangover to the mix.'

She laughed then. 'Yes, Dad.' It was a joke, but it held more than a ring of truth. Dennis, and his wife, Hetty, had taken her under their wing from the moment she'd stepped into their office, a naïve eighteen-year-old with a big voice and an even bigger dream. She'd never have made it without them.

'Hey, I'm not that old!' he protested with a chuckle. 'Well, not quite anyway. Enjoy the rest of your evening, Aurora. I'll see you tomorrow.'

The call ended, leaving Aurora staring at the unanswered message from Nick. With a sigh of regret, she closed the app and set her phone back down on the table. There was no point starting things up with him when she was leaving the country and didn't plan to be back for at least six months. It wouldn't be fair to either of them.

Trying not to think too hard about the pretty little village of Mermaids Point and the man with the laughing eyes, she wandered from the living room into the bathroom to run herself a hot bath. As she slid into the soothing cocoon of hot water and bubbles, she allowed herself one final thought about what might have been. *Merry Christmas, Nick, and I hope the new year brings happiness ... for both of us.*

ACKNOWLEDGMENTS

Huge thanks to my brilliant editor, Sarah Ritherdon, who when I sent her an email titled Good/Terrible Idea not only read it but gave me the space to figure out whether it was indeed a good or terrible idea.

Extra special thanks to everyone who stepped up at short notice to help make this happen:

Alice Moore who designed the beautiful cover (as well as the equally gorgeous one for *Autumn Dreams*).

Sue Lamprell who guided me so expertly through the Copy and Proof Edits.

Nia, Megan, Claire and all the Boldwood team behind the scenes who sorted out production and marketing in record time.

Finally, thanks to each and every reader who has already made the Mermaids Point series such a success. Your lovely comments and feedback make it all worthwhile and this book is my little Christmas gift to you. Thank you xx

A NOTE FROM SARAH BENNETT

Dear Reader,

Whether this is your first visit to Mermaids Point, or you are a returning visitor, I hope you have enjoyed this peek behind the festive curtains at what everyone is up to. If you are looking for more from the characters featured, each couple has – or will have – their own full length story.

The series started in March 2021 with Jake and Laurie in *Summer Kisses at Mermaids Point* where Jake arrives to investigate a series of mysterious mermaid sightings. His hunt for the truth is distracted by Laurie, the owner of a local café, though he has his work cut out if he wants her to break her cardinal rule which is never getting involved with a visitor to the Point.

We returned to Mermaids Point in September 2021 for *Autumn Dreams at Mermaids Point*. There's a new doctor in town in the shape of Tom who arrives with his two teenage children hoping a fresh start will help bring them closer together following a tragic loss. The new surgery comes complete with a receptionist and live-in housekeeper – Nerissa. It's not the right time for either of them, but will the mermaids weave their magic and bring them together?

On our next visit, which is planned for Spring 2022, you'll find out more about Alex and Ivy as he moves to Mermaids Point and takes over the local bookshop. Will he let Ivy in on the secret he's been keeping, and will she be able to forgive him for stealing her dream?

Finally, we'll be back in Mermaids Point in time for Christmas 2022 where Nick finds the last person he expects to see again turning up on his doorstep. Aurora's back in town, but what's the real motive behind her visit?

I'm so excited to share all this and more with you. Wishing you and yours a very Merry Christmas and a peaceful, prosperous New Year,

Love, Sarah x

MORE FROM SARAH BENNETT

We hope you enjoyed reading *Christmas Surprises at Mermaids Point*. If you did, please leave a review.

If you'd like to gift a copy, this book is also available as an ebook, digital audio download and audiobook CD.

Sign up to Sarah Bennett's mailing list for news, competitions and updates on future books.

https://bit.ly/SarahBennettNewsletter

Summer Kisses at Mermaids Point, another warm, escapist, feel-good story from Sarah Bennett, is available now.

ABOUT THE AUTHOR

Sarah Bennett is the bestselling author of several romantic fiction trilogies including those set in *Butterfly Cove* and *Lavender Bay*. Born and raised in a military family she is happily married to her own Officer and when not reading or writing enjoys sailing the high seas.

Visit Sarah's website: https://sarahbennettauthor.wordpress.com/

Follow Sarah on social media:

- facebook.com/SarahBennettAuthor
- twitter.com/Sarahlou_writes
- bookbub.com/authors/sarah-bennett-b4a48ebb-a5c3-4c39-b59a-09aa9idc7cfa
- instagram.com/sarahlbennettauthor

ABOUT BOLDWOOD BOOKS

Boldwood Books is a fiction publishing company seeking out the best stories from around the world.

Find out more at www.boldwoodbooks.com

Sign up to the Book and Tonic newsletter for news, offers and competitions from Boldwood Books!

http://www.bit.ly/bookandtonic

We'd love to hear from you, follow us on social media:

facebook.com/BookandTonic

twitter.com/BoldwoodBooks

instagram.com/BookandTonic

Printed in Great Britain
by Amazon